BUCHANAN
CALLS
THE SHOTS

BUCHANAN
CALLS
THE SHOTS

Jonas Ward

A FAWCETT GOLD MEDAL BOOK

Fawcett Publications, Inc., Greenwich, Connecticut

ONE

THEY RODE in from the east, Buchanan up on Nightshade and Coco Bean astride a fine roan called Champion, threading their way past herds being held in readiness for drives northward. They could see the lights of Fort Worth in the distance and knew the town would be full of drifters, gamblers, ladies of the evening, and sharp-eyed men making deals for land and cattle and wheat and corn and whatever lent itself to profit. It was getting on to twilight, and they were in no great hurry.

Coco said, "You been up the trails plenty, ain't you?"

"Plenty. Too often." Buchanan was six-feet-four-inches, looming tall in the saddle, a battle-scarred giant. He was sandy-haired, with wide-spaced greenish eyes. He weighed two hundred and fifty pounds, give or take a few. His rifle was buckled into a scabbard, he wore no six-gun. Buchanan was a man of peace.

Coco Bean was black, with wooly, close-cropped hair and a few marks of battle, but not as many as might be expected. Coco had survived over a hundred bare-knuckle prize fights without a loss. He was shorter than Buchanan and somewhat lighter, but he was quick as a puma, and his strength was that of the righteous.

"Long ride, hard work," Coco said.

"You been on the trails? I didn't know that."

Coco replied hastily, "Naw, I never. I only heard."

"You're lucky. It's a dog's life." Buchanan paused, then grinned. "Lot of satisfaction when you bring 'em through, though. Abilene, that was once a place. Nowadays Dodge is wild. Friend of mine, Luke Short, he's operatin' in Dodge."

"I'd rather just be a fighter," Coco said. "You think we'll have a real big purse in Fort Worth?"

"Not only a big purse. You beat Corcoran and you'll make those newspaper people perk up. You'll get a championship bout or I'm a Dutchman."

Buchanan was Scottish and he wore a hundred scars gained in battles he had tried to evade. He was a man of the West, a veteran of the frontier. He had experienced almost every phase of the western ways and tomorrow he might face a new angle. It was all the same to Tom Buchanan, a happy man on a tall horse.

Coco said, "I dunno. They don't want to fight a black man, them big fellas from the East. They had a lotta trouble with Molyneaux and a couple others. They got a new Negro name of Jackson, I hear, just a boy, scares 'em all."

"I know." It was a sad fact. Buchanan firmly believed that Coco Bean was the best bare-fist fighter in the world, but it was a hard thing to prove. "Sometimes I think maybe we ought to go to England or France. I got the money—or I can get it any time. Make a name over there, come back and call you the 'European Champ.'"

Coco asked, "Can they bleach your skin in Europe?"

There was no answer to that. Coco had made his living taking on all comers with side bets to fatten the meager purses. When Buchanan was in his corner, he managed to live well. When they were separated by force of circumstance, he had not done so well, due to the shenanigans of promoters and other crooks.

"Never mind," Coco went on. "We do in Corcoran,

collect and mebbe take a trip to Frisco, huh? Haven't been to Frisco lately."

"New Orleans softened me up enough," said Buchanan. "I got to get under the stars and up in the hills and catch a fish and shoot a bear."

"Okay. You do that." Coco snorted. "Guns. Killin' things. Always the guns."

"A bearskin would look good in the Buttons house," said Buchanan. "The kid could play with it."

"Well . . . ." The Buttons baby was Coco's favorite playmate and friend. The child's parents owned a fine house in New Mexico. "But I don't like them guns. I will be scared of guns all my life."

"Guns opened the West. Guns make some kinda law— maybe not good law, but some kind. If I didn't have to carry 'em, it would be okay with me," Buchanan said. "But right now, lemme tell you, without 'em we would be long dead."

And for this Coco had no answer. It was something they worried about, each in his own way. There had been one occasion when Coco had handled a rifle, shooting at people who deserved to be shot at. He did not like to think about it. There had been times when he and Buchanan had been caught without weapons and had to battle for their lives, barely escaping extinction. It was a problem never quite solved in that era of western civilization.

They were still miles from the city when they came to a scattered herd of cattle. Buchanan reined in, frowning in the gathering dusk.

"There should be a herder right here," he said. "Somebody don't know how to handle beef on the hoof."

"None of our business," said Coco. He added, "Is it?"

"The chuck wagon's too far away." Buchanan stood high in his saddle for a moment, staring. "I swear, there ain't a rider in sight. Could be somethin' wrong . . . Wait! Look yonder."

A pony bucked, then slung sideways and ran. Aboard without a saddle, using the end of rope attached to a hackamore, a tall, husky youth kicked at its ribs. The

7

horse finally understood and began to run. It headed straight for Buchanan and Coco.

When the boy could be clearly distinguished in the gathering dusk, they saw that he was shock-headed, attired in Levi's, worn boots and a torn shirt. One eye was rapidly closing and blood ran from the corner of his mouth. He yanked the pony to a sliding halt.

"What's goin' on there, youngster?" Buchanan demanded.

"Lu . . . She sent me lookin' for help . . . Lu, you know, Lulu Lacy. She said maybe a big galoot named Buchanan might be . . ."

"Where's she at? What's doin'?" They were already riding back in the tracks of the lunging horse.

"Bull Skagg," gasped the boy. "They got her in a bind, him, Morgan, Krause and Gotch. They all turned on her. They walloped me and she yelled to ride out. She had that li'l ol' gun . . ."

Coco said, "Another lady? Tom, you know some lady in every town and camp and reservation west of the damn Mississippi. And they're all trouble."

Buchanan was riding ahead by now, Nightshade hitting the familiar stride which had covered so many miles in so little time. There was a tent beyond the deserted chuck wagon. From inside came the sound of loud voices, then the pop of a small bore pistol. A woman screamed.

Then Buchanan arrived. It was a big tent, the sort used by the owners or visitors while holding a herd, circular and high around a middle pole. When he came down from the saddle, he noticed that one side bulged with the weight of people within.

He paused a moment at the flap, getting his bearings. There were four men and there was Lu Lacy. The men had her by the arms and were trying to secure her legs, which were long, shapely and active. She was a tall girl and kicked well, and her language was enough to burn the ears off an ordinary citizen. Her dress was ripped and her high, full bosom heaved with rage and, more than likely, fear. Buchanan was not certain about the fear.

He took the nearest man, who seemed to be enjoying

the scene in the half dark, and spun him around. He hit with a full-armed swing to the middle—at a point somewhat below the man's belt. There was a gulping, moaning noise. The man doubled over as he fell.

The second of the quartet turned around to see what was going on. Buchanan hit him with a chop to the neck and sent him to the ground, where he landed on his face.

The lady who was known as Lu yelled, "Buchanan! Get 'em, Buchanan!"

The pair who were holding her let go, and she sprawled on the dirt floor of the tent. One of them made a quick move to the back of his neck and came out with a fourteen-inch Bowie knife. The light in the tent was uncertain and Buchanan stood a moment, weighing his decision.

The man without the knife dove low. He was squat and heavy. His shoulder struck Buchanan at the knees and knocked him down. The knife expert pounced. Lu shrieked.

Coco was coming through the tent flap. He took two steps and caught the wrist of the man with the Bowie. Buchanan kicked out and nailed the second assailant at the kneecap. Lu scrambled around on the floor and found her .32 caliber gun. She yelled, "I got it, Buchanan. Lemme handle them. I got five shots. Four'll do to kill the bastards."

Coco was swinging his arm. He let go at the sound of the word "gun" and sent the man flying out of the tent. He ran to Lu and closed his big hand over her fist and took away the gun.

Out in the open there were sounds of battle. Buchanan righted himself and peered. The blond youth was whacking Coco's victim with both hands, raking him across the face. It seemed fair enough revenge. Buchanan returned to the tent.

As it rapidly became darker on the Texas plain, the bruised warriors were making an effort to depart the scene. Buchanan blocked the path. Coco had to hit one of them in the ribs to keep him quiet.

Buchanan said, "Lu, it's a change to find people

raisin' hell with you. Mostly it's the t'other way around."

"I'll kill every damn one of them," she vowed. "The sons of no mothers! They wasn't born! They crawled out from under rocks!"

"How come you're messin' with them?"

"Either let me kill 'em or get them outa here," she said. "I tell you, Buchanan, I'm about to explode."

"You are comin' apart some." Her dress was ripped away from rounded shoulders and blossoming bosom. She leaned hard against Buchanan. She was quaking. He said, "Name 'em and we'll run 'em. Then we'll talk."

She pointed a quivering finger. "Bull Skagg, the one you hit first . . . Monk Morgan, which Kid is beating up on, I hope . . . Butch Krause, that ugly . . . Bowie Gotch, the bastard with the knife."

Buchanan said, "Light me a lantern so I'll recognize them if I ever see 'em again. Coco, take their weapons and walk 'em outdoors and hold them a couple minutes."

Coco looked at the Bowie in his hand. He muttered, "Don't like pig-stickers, neither. But it's better'n a gun."

Buchanan helped the shaking Lu with a lantern. The glow filled the tent. She was too disturbed to attempt to cover herself. She said, "I got about five hundred head of cattle together. Ran outa money. Skagg agreed to drive 'em to Dodge. I couldn't raise the dough to pay advance wages and he came at me. I talked back. They turned on me like you saw."

At the tent flap, Skagg turned and said, "Goddam whore, she's a liar."

Buchanan cuffed him with open hand, as an adult would chastise a child. Skagg went to his knees, his face turning blood-red. His right hand dropped to his belt where a gun nested in its holster. Coco kicked the hand away and Buchanan plucked out the revolver. Coco swung around with the Bowie still in his grasp and the trouble-makers all instinctively raised their hands.

Buchanan said, "I've heard enough for now. Do these people own horses? Saddles?"

"Yes," she said.

"The boy know about all that?"

10

"Kid? Yes, Kid knows."

"That his name, Kid?"

"He's got no other. Kid Texas, they call him. He's a good boy."

Skagg growled something beneath his breath, looked nervously at Buchanan and did not continue.

Buchanan went to the flap of the tent. The fourth man lay in the dirt, snoring. The Kid was washing himself at a water basin atop a crate.

Buchanan asked, "You got enough licks in?"

"I wore myself out," said the Kid. He had a wide grin and white teeth. He was young enough to be all elbows and wrists and ham-like hands.

"How old are you, anyway?" Buchanan asked.

"Fifteen. I been up the trail once. Almost."

"Didn't make it, eh?"

"I wasn't even fourteen. Pea green," he confessed. "Bull Skagg, he fired me."

Coco had them lined up. The man on the ground awakened, stared about in the reflected light from the tent. He reached for his gun. His holster was empty.

Skagg muttered, "Damn kid was no damn good . . ." He bit the sentence off, flinching away from Buchanan. He was a big man, wide in the shoulder but now, thoroughly cowed.

Buchanan separated their weapons, ejecting shells. He held out his hand for belts. He emptied those, stacking the ammunition neatly on the crate where Kid Texas now stood guard, beaming through his bruises.

"You catch up your mounts," Buchanan said. "You get your guns back. You ride. You keep on ridin'. You don't make a sound to disturb the cattle you haven't taken care of. Understood?"

Skagg said, "I understand, all right. And I got a good memory, Buchanan."

"Uh-huh. I'll let that pass. Let's see you start."

The man called Bowie Gotch stopped beside Coco, glaring at him. "I want my knife."

"No," said Buchanan.

"I got a right to my knife."

11

"See me in Fort Worth," Buchanan told him. "We'll talk to Marshal Doud."

"Damn Marshal Doud. I want my knife!"

Buchanan took one step, closing his fist. "You uglies did harm to a friend of mine. I'm lettin' you off easy. Just for now. I'll see you in Fort Worth."

Skagg, already in motion, called, "Come on, Gotch. I got ideas. Come on!"

Buchanan watched them. He mounted Nightshade and followed them. He saw them ride for the lights of the not too distant city. Then he returned to the tent.

He said, "Kid, you and Coco go out there and bring that herd in where it belongs. Stay with it until I get things straight around here. Okay?"

"You betcha," said Texas Kid.

Coco looked wounded. "Hey, Tom. Me? Rustle cattle?"

"You don't rustle 'em. You don't even hustle 'em. Let the boy show you. Your horse is cattle-wise. Just set in the saddle and all will be fine."

"But I ain't no cowboy!"

"Herder," Buchanan said. "Herder is the word. Or drover. Only now you're herdin' em in and holdin' them awhile. Maybe all night."

"But we got to get to town and see about Corcoran and all!"

"Coco, there's a lady in trouble here."

Coco frowned. "I'll be damned. I purely don't like it."

The Kid had brought up the wiry pony, now complete with bridle and a rundown, ratty saddle. He rode as though born on a horse. He yipped, "C'mon there, man! Let's git goin'."

Coco grumbled once more, then followed. Buchanan shook his head. If someone started a stampede . . . He didn't want to think about it. He went into the tent.

Lu Macy had put on a robe. She was sitting on an apple box, her knees crossed. Her shoulders were hunched. She was completely disconsolate.

Buchanan said, "Okay, what you been up to this time? Outside of consortin' with blacklegs of the lowest count?"

"Tryin' to get out of the dance halls and the gamblin'

hells," she retorted. "I told you that in El Paso last time I saw you."

"You said you wanted to get out. Then you ran off with that Handsome Harry fella."

"Jerry, his name was. Jerry Schumacher."

"You had a grubstake then."

"I know."

He had dimples, Buchanan remembered.

"He ran into a cold deck in Virginia City. Another tinhorn shot him through the right side dimple."

"And your stake was gone."

"Long gone, by then. I made it to Dodge and dealt faro. Then I heard they were gatherin' the herds down here and I saw the profits bein' made on beef. So I came down."

"With all that cash for five-hundred head?"

"Well, I bought a table in Johnstone's. You know Kak."

"Good old Kak. Rents out his poker tables. Scared to take a chance."

"I had a room upstairs, it was okay. I made out."

"Uh-huh," said Buchanan. "Who sold you the herd?"

"Fella named Derick Demetrius. You heard of him? Greek descent, curly hair, lousy rich?"

"Dimples?"

"Well . . . One. He's the one found Skagg and them for me, damn his soul."

Buchanan said, "You ain't always real smart, are you, Lu?"

"Nope. I bet they were plannin' to run the herd up to Wyoming, rebrand it and sell it off."

"Well, I noted you got that Cross I brand. It can be made into Double L real easy. But then none of 'em are real safe."

"The double-crossin' son! That kid tried to tell me and I wouldn't listen."

"What about the kid?"

"Texas? He just came into town. Swamped at Johnstone's, then got a job in a stable, Haussling's stable, he really knows horses. Big damn kid, I like him."

"Dimples," said Buchanan. "I noticed."

"Now you quit that! After Schumacher . . . Never mind. Texas Kid won't tell anything about his name, his past, nothin'. But he's been good to me."

"I'll buy that. Now, he said you sent him lookin' in case I was comin' in. How'd you know that?"

"The fight with Corcoran. Everybody knows you and Coco Bean are friends and it was to be a real big bout."

"Did you say 'was to be'?"

"Didn't you know? The governor hates fights."

"He wasn't supposed to know until too late."

"Somebody squealed. The Rangers are in town."

"Oh, Lord, the damn Rangers. I thought Marshal Doud would be in charge."

"He can't fight the Rangers."

"I know." Buchanan scratched his head. "Now tell me, were you goin' up the trail with the herd your own self?"

"I was thinkin' about it. I got some clothes and things at Johnstone's."

"You're crazy, I know that. But I didn't think you were that crazy."

"Cook—he got drunk and wandered off," she said. "It's too late to hire another. Too late to hire a crew." She drooped, despondent. "I'm in a hell of a fix. But I can ride and I can cook and I can drive a team. And I can shoot a damn gun if I have to."

He looked at her in sympathy. She had high cheekbones and wide-spaced eyes. Her mouth was full-lipped, and she bore none of the scars of the dance hall girls. She must have come from strong, resilient stock, he thought.

He said, "Can you manage to help Coco and the Kid tonight? Stand watch and all? Feed 'em in the saddle?"

"The herd'll stand in graze easy enough. I can do it."

"Tell Coco what you heard about the fight. Just stick tight. I'll ride in, pick up your stuff at Kak's place, and talk to Doud."

"Then what?"

"Maybe I can round you up some men. Or you could join one of the amalgamations goin' up to Dodge, a big herd."

"They're all gone," she said sadly. "It'll be tough

enough, tailin' them, takin' their dust and their leavin's."

"You gonna trust me or should I look around for some galoot with dimples?" he demanded.

She came close, looking up at him. "Tom?"

"Uh-huh?"

"If you'd said one word. Just one."

"Now, you're just telling me that."

"You know it's the truth. I never would've gone off with anybody if you'd just given me a damn hint."

He said uncomfortably, "Now Lu. You know me. I always got places to go and things to do. You pretty as a speckled pup, but I'm a man searchin' for peace and never findin' it."

"But you're goin' to help me."

"Well, sure, Lu. I'll do what I can."

She lifted her face as innocently as a child, and he kissed her. She was a fine figure of a woman, he had always known. He lifted her briefly off her feet, kissed her once more, set her down again.

"You do like I say," he admonished her. "I better get movin' and see what's up."

He went outside and gathered the ammunition he had taken from the four men. He put it in a heap and turned the box over and stowed it away. It might come in handy, he thought.

He knew men like Skagg and his followers. He had been up and down and around and about with them all his life. They were dangerous as long as they were loose upon the land. They would be a threat to Lu and to himself until the issue was settled, which could take a week, a month, a year, or even a decade.

It would take a heap of hard work and the most careful vigilance to get Lu's comparatively small herd to Dodge City in time for the buying season. The profit would not be great with things the way they were, he thought.

He whistled and Nightshade came. In the near distance he could see that Kid Texas and Coco were slowly moving the cattle into a holding pattern. The big young boy seemed to know the business.

Coco would be devastated—and broke—if the fight

with Corcoran did not go through, he knew. Coco was a quick man with a dollar when he got into a city like New Orleans. Buchanan, however, could always save a bit of money.

There was plenty to think about as he rode through the night.

TWO

WITH THE HERDS gone up the trail, Fort Worth was settling down, but it was still lively enough for any man. Buchanan put up his horse at Haussling's stable. The owner was a straw-haired German.

"*Ja, wohl*, the poy was a goodt poy," he said. "Keed Texas, hu? Very goodt mitt der horses. Honest like der day."

Buchanan said, "Here's a dollar. I may pull out pronto, but I want a good mess of oats and I want him curried. Okay?"

"I do it my own self. Keed, he is out there? On de plain?"

"He'll be all right."

"A goodt poy. It is nice to find a goodt poy."

"Uh-huh," said Buchanan. "Gettin' to be a rarity, too."

He walked down the main street. He knew Johnstone's. It was big and bright and gaudy, but if you were onto the people who bought the tables, you could pick and choose your own poison. Some of them were honest.

17

Before he came to the entrance, Marshal Doud stepped from an alleyway and put out a hand.

"Howdy," Buchanan said. "How are you?"

"Purely disgusted. You heard about the fight?"

"I heard the Rangers are in town."

"Damn their souls. I'm plumb sorry down to my boots, Tom. Corcoran already left town."

"No chance, then."

"Not a smidgin. Corcoran heard so much about Coco from the boys that he was relieved to get out, I do believe."

Buchanan nodded. "We might've taken it to El Paso, where we could dodge across the Rio if the Rangers got tough."

"Right smart distance, though." The marshal, a lean and lanky man, tipped back his sombrero. "Anything I can do for you, Tom?"

"Lu Lacy and her beef, out yonder. What do you know about the deal?"

"Demetrius, the bastid," said Doud promptly. "Took her savin's and loaded Bull Skagg and some others on her. You know Skagg?"

"I do now," said Buchanan. "He's wearin' my brand."

"Good! What's Lu gonna do?"

"Are there any drovers left in town?"

"None worth a fiddler's fit. Demetrius goes out in the mornin', about the last of them. This is like fare-thee-well night. And I'll be damn glad when it's over."

"Better'n being in Dodge when they get up there after the months on the trail."

"Maybe. But Kansas don't have no damn Rangers." The Marshal was bitter. He brightened. "Hey, Tom. There's a fella named Porado. Little guy, slick as an eel. Tricky but a loyal little bastid. He could mebbe help Lu."

"Porado? Does he know the trail?"

"Like a book."

"Then why ain't he on it with a big herd?"

"He's only got a couple hundred head of his own. Came across, wetbacks no doubt. Anyway, he branded 'em and then couldn't catch on with anybody. He's got Dude Healy and Dutch Charlie workin' for him. Got a decent cavvy, too."

"Tricky, eh?"

"Well, tell you the truth, he's done time. But he's got good points, Tom."

"Where can I find this Porado?"

"I'll see that he gets to Johnstone's right quick."

"Is Kak still chicken-hearted and smart?"

"He don't change none."

Buchanan said, "I got to get Lu's things."

Doud whistled. "You mean she's goin' up the trail?"

"Has Porado got a cook?"

"Hell, you wouldn't want his kinda cook. Chile and beans every day for breakfast."

"Then Lu's goin' up the trail. It's been done by a woman before now."

"I know." Marshal Doud hesitated. "But . . . well, you know."

"What do I know?"

"Bad luck. It's always bad luck when a woman's on a trail drive."

"Superstition," said Buchanan. "Silly damn stuff."

"Well . . . So long as you ain't goin' along," said Doud.

"Uh-huh," Buchanan replied. "I better see Kak and be on my way."

"You are goin' up the trail after all these years?" demanded the marshal.

Buchanan said, "What the hell would I do that for?"

Doud, turning away, grinned. "That Lu ain't exactly somethin' to sneeze at. Anyway, you need anything, you yell. I'll be 'round."

"I'll yell loud enough. See you later."

He walked toward the gambling hall-saloon known as "Johnstone's Place." His mind was moving slowly now. Go up the trail? He had no intention of driving a bunch of damn temperamental cattle up a long and winding and exhausting trail to Kansas. He had been to Kansas. He didn't need to go there again. His adopted home was the high plain of southwest New Mexico. He had interests there and friends.

Still, there was Lu Lacy. She was a young woman, he was well aware, who had been a victim of the country and the times, born in east Texas, not far from his own birthplace, she had lost her parents in a flood. No one had been willing to give a home to a hoydenish teen-ager, and she had too much pride to make a marriage of convenience, to become a slave to a farmer or rancher anxious only for a warm bed and many children to do the chores.

So she had drifted westward by one means or another. Without schooling, she had used her naturally bright wit and her physical charms to get a foothold in the society of independent women of the frontier. She had long, sensitive fingers and quick hands, and she quickly developed a nose for games of chance. This had put her at the top of the heap, made her a person to be reckoned with.

Her weakness for handsome men—"dimples", as Buchanan called them—was disastrous. Twice it had led her into bankruptcy. This was a third chance, this venture into the cattle business. It might well be her last, Buchanan thought. She was certainly in danger of losing everything; she needed a lot of help. He was meditative as he entered the large establishment of Kak Johnstone.

The place boasted two bars, each long, curving and shiny, manned by white-aproned huskies who were noted for their ability—and willingness—to fight. They were, people snickered, stand-ins for Johnstone, the little man with no nerve who managed somehow to survive in a rough world.

Buchanan stood inside the street entrance and took in the scene. The place was full, the mood was gay. The season was ending that night and those remaining would take every advantage. Men drank, all the tables were occupied, the roulette wheels spun, glittering in the light of fifty chandeliers. Mirrors reflected the scene, heightened the effect. Girls moved languidly among the patrons, their chests almost completely nude, their skirts short.

Kak Johnstone was at the farthest end of a bar. Glancing right and left, Buchanan made for him. Two burly barkeeps moved parallel with Buchanan.

Johnstone peered, then grinned in relief. He spoke to his cohorts. "It's okay. Buchanan's a friend."

"Howdy, Kak. Let's not be too friendly too fast," Buchanan suggested. "I got questions."

"Okay, you got questions. Would I lie to you?" Johnstone had a high voice and a habit of looking over the shoulder of the person he was addressing. He had squinty eyes and wore a drooping, carefully tended mustache.

"You'd lie to your mother. And you've done so," said Buchanan. "Now tell me, which table is Lu Lacy's?"

"Not 'is' but 'was.' Demetrius bought her out," said Johnstone promptly. He jerked a quick thumb, discreetly, a bit fearfully. "Right there. Derick Demetrius."

It was a central table in a good spot. Lu must have done a fine business at it, Buchanan thought. The man named Demetrius was easy to spot. He dominated the area about him, the people within his aura. He was dark as tanbark with an olive tint to his skin. He had round, bright eyes and curly black hair. He sported a diamond on the third finger of each hand. His teeth were very white. There was no real humor in his smile.

Lounging nearby, but not gambling, were Bull Skagg, Butch Krause, Monk Morgan and Bowie Gotch. That they were attendants to Demetrius was in no way a surprise to Buchanan. They had seen him and were trying to act nonchalant. Skagg touched Demetrius, drew a frown, leaned and spoke in his ear. Demetrius turned and stared openly.

Buchanan stared back. The man was bulky, with a few rolls of fat at his chin and around the middle. He seemed out of place in a western frontier city. He wore gambler's black with a splash of color in the vest, and a string tie, dark red like spilled blood. His black hair curled about the white collar of his shirt. There was a weapon under his left arm, Buchanan saw, and probably one up his sleeve. A man like Demetrius neither took chances nor obeyed inconvenient local laws.

Kak Johnstone said in his reedy, nervous voice, "Now don't you go to startin' nothin', Tom. You know it upsets me no end."

"I'll want Lu's things," said Buchanan. "And I'll want to know if it's the truth that he paid for the table."

"He paid."

"The right price?"

"It was what she took for it, Tom. Jeez, don't start breakin' things now, will ya, please?"

"Why Kak, you know I'm a peaceable man." He motioned to the big bartender. He poured from a proffered bottle. "One thing about you. Never knew you to serve bad whiskey."

"Please, I know you put them marks on Skagg and the others. They come in here askin' questions and all."

"And you answered them, didn't you, Kak?"

"I hadda, didn't I? Demetrius, he said to answer. He 'bout owns the town right now, since the others have gone up the trail and wherever."

"Uh-huh." He couldn't imagine Demetrius or anyone like him dwarfing Shanghai Pierce or Charley Goodnight or any of that ilk.

"Well, he's rollin' in money. And money talks, you know that."

Buchanan said, "Trouble is, I never could understand the lingo. Get one of your flunkies to bring down Lu's things, will you? And I mean everything."

A slender, medium-sized man was edging his way down the bar. He was dark and he wore clothing which proclaimed him ready for the trail. He was listening to Buchanan's every word. Over at the poker table which once belonged to Lu, the man with the diamond rings had shifted his gaze and now was glowering at the newcomer.

Buchanan asked without turning his head, "Your name Porado, maybe?"

"That is my name." He spoke precisely, with very little accent. His face was sharply cut, his eyes deep brown, intelligent. His lips were thin and did not move when he spoke. "Buchanan?"

"Yes."

"Doud sent me."

"It ain't exactly a good time to be here," Buchanan

told him, speaking as if to Kak Johnstone. "Say somethin', Kak."

"Uh—the swamper'll get Lu's things."

Porado spoke again. "If it's Demetrius, as I believe, then go ahead and do what you must."

"I'm a peaceable man. Those people, they're not peaceable."

"Doud tells me you are unarmed."

"Like I say, I never look for trouble. Trouble looks for me, sometimes."

Porado said, "Be very careful, then."

Buchanan still looked at Kak Johnstone. "I'm always careful. Right?"

"Sure, Tom. Sure, you are," said Johnstone. He was a little pale now. In the mirror, Buchanan saw Demetrius arise from the table. The quartet headed by Bull Skagg moved behind him as he approached. A silence fell over the saloon, filled with fear, anticipation, and curiosity. Buchanan turned, hooking his elbows on the bar, towering over the scene. Johnstone vanished, his bartender stood stock still, one hand on a shotgun that hung beneath the mahogany.

Porado moved as though on wheels. He seemed to dissolve as Demetrius and his men formed a half circle around Buchanan.

The dark man with the curly hair was shorter than Buchanan, but possibly wider. He was thick through the body, hard and muscular. His arms were short and powerful, his hands large, his fingers long. He stared up at Buchanan, deliberately arrogant.

"You want to butt into things not your business, eh?" The voice was silky and laden with menace.

Buchanan looked deep into the burning eyes. "You mean these low-down rats? They workin' for you?"

Demetrius retorted, "That is my business. See that you remain out of it."

Buchanan raised his voice, thundering. "These damn no-goods were attackin' a woman. You know what that means in this country? A hangin' tree, mister."

There was a growl which ran around the room. De-

23

metrius wheeled, the gleam in his eye turned to calculation. He stared at Bull Skagg.

"Attacking a woman? Is this true?"

"Naw. He's a liar!"

Buchanan reached out one hand. He caught Skagg beneath the chin, clawing his fingers into the base of the jaw. The man's arms waved, he tried to kick out.

Buchanan let him put a shin against heel so that he howled, then slammed him against Monk Morgan, who fell into Butch Krause, who tripped the charging Bowie Gotch. Once more they were piled at Buchanan's feet.

Demetrius reached under his coat for the shoulder gun. From behind him, Porado appeared as though by magic. In his right hand was a shining, curved blade. He held it against Demetrius's throat.

Buchanan was watching the rest of the crowd. They were all retreating from the action. Two men in sombreros and sober garments came through the front door. They wore badges recognizable to every Texan.

Porado said to Buchanan, "Rangers. Doud sent them. I'll be leaving now."

Demetrius said violently but quietly, "You will die soon, Porado. Very soon."

But Porado seemed to have a mystical quality for disappearing. He was gone.

Buchanan said, "Demetrius, seems to me you talk a lot." He shoved the man aside, stepped over recumbent bodies and went toward the Rangers. He greeted them in turn.

"Bell? . . . Sands? . . . Howdy."

"Howdy, Tom. You got trouble?"

"No real trouble."

"Want to make a complaint?"

"Uh-huh."

"Just name it."

"I'll make it in person."

Sands, the taller Ranger, said, "Now, Tom. Not in Fort Worth. You know the captain."

"I know him. He knows me, too."

"Try and keep it peaceable around here, Tom. What

24

with that fight bein' called off." He paused, then asked, "It is called off, ain't it? I mean, the governor, he's dead set."

Buchanan said, "It's off. Corcoran left town."

Sergeant Bell asked, "Wasn't there a fella named Porado in here a minute ago?"

"Porado? What's he look like?"

Sands said hurriedly, "Never mind, Tom. Forget it. Porado's pulled a couple things. Demetrius, he's been hollerin' up a storm."

"Demetrius will get his storm if he crosses my path again. And that goes for the length of the trail to Dodge."

"You goin' up the trail?" asked Sands, surprised.

"I wasn't," Buchanan said. "Porado did me a favor this evenin'. I understand he needs help. And there's another herd out yonder that has to be moved."

"Just watch yourself," Sands said. "Demetrius can be real bad. Real bad, Tom."

"He's pizen," said Bell. "Plain pizen."

"There's antidotes for poison," Buchanan said. Demetrius had gone, along with Skagg and the others. He had contracted a debt there, he knew. Ranger Bell's warning was apropos. The trail would be even less a picnic than under ordinary circumstances.

"Just take it easy around here," Sands insisted. "The captain, he'll be real mad at us if you start one of your rangdoodles."

"Nobody here to fight with," Buchanan said. Johnstone was leading an old man and a saloon girl, who between them were toting a trunk, several packages and folded garments frilly with lace and bright with gewgaws. "Got to take these belongin's out to Lu Lacy."

"Lu? Oh me, oh my, you have bought yourself trouble," said Ranger Bell. "Her and Demetrius had a big fight."

"I heard," Buchanan told them. He waited, knowing they would not press him further.

Sands said, "Well, good luck, Tom. Sorry about the prizefight. I had a bet down on Coco."

"So long," said Buchanan. "Thanks for the help."

They departed and he turned to Johnstone. He looked at the gowns, shook his head.

"They're hers," said Johnstone. "She paid for 'em."

"Keep 'em for her," said Buchanan. "Bring the rest of it outside. And Kak, whatever you tell Demetrius and them, don't lie any. I wouldn't want to hear you told things about me outa school."

"Who, me?" Johnstone raised his hands in horror. "I'm your friend, Tom."

"Uh-huh. A couple more like you and I don't need no enemies." He followed the old man onto the street and piled the possessions of Lu Lacy on the walk. He leaned against the building and waited with confidence. He was rewarded by the appearance of Porado.

"I have a wagon." The man spoke careful English, sometimes oddly accented but always correct. He picked up the packages and put a hand on the trunk. "If you will."

Buchanan waved him away and lifted the heavy trunk to his shoulder without effort.

"Need the exercise. Been loafin' around New Orleans and like o' that. Man gets soft."

In the light from the saloon a fleeting smile crossed the face of Porado, but he spoke solemnly, "As you say, Buchanan. The wagon is around the next corner."

There was very little light on the side street. Porado whistled, and a converted buckboard pulled out of an alley. There was a tall man on the seat and a fat man ready with a rifle at the head of the team of horses.

Porado said, "This is Buchanan. He's going with us."

The men were silent. Buchanan put the trunk in the wagon body, which was almost full of supplies. Porado put the bag in beside the trunk and walked a few steps with him.

Buchanan said, "Got a horse at the stable."

"I know. Doud told me some," Porado said.

"Doud a friend of yours?"

"He sent me to the pen."

"Uh-huh," Buchanan said. "Way you talked in Johnstone's, I would've known."

"You learn in jail if you want to. Dude Healy there is the driver. Dutch Charlie is the fat man. They didn't learn much. But they kept the wolves from my back. Jail is full of wolf packs."

"Two-legged ones. I heard," Buchanan said

"We are trying to get this small herd to Dodge."

Buchanan said, "You got a brand registered?"

"Flying P."

It would have been rude to ask any further questions. It was none of his business if any of the three were wanted by the law.

Buchanan said, "You know where Lu Lacy is camped?"

"We know."

"I'll be right along, soon as I pick up my horse," said Buchanan. "You want to throw your herd into hers, go ahead."

"We're not in that much of a hurry," Porado said. "They've all got a start on us by now. We may as well take it easy. We can sell seven hundred and fifty head for sure, when we get to Dodge, hers and ours."

"If we get to Dodge." The tall man spoke from the wagon seat. "If they don't jump us by the time we hit the Red."

Buchanan shrugged. "Demetrius will jump us. We know it. So we'll be ready for him."

The fat man called Dutch Charlie said, "Yah. Twenty men, he'll have. And maybe some Injuns."

Buchanan told him, "So long as we know, that'll be okay."

Porado said, "We'd better get along."

Buchanan waved and turned and walked back to the main street and down toward the livery stable. He had just sent three ex-convicts to deliver Lu Lacy's belongings. It seemed ridiculous but he had seen stranger situations.

Marshal Doud was waiting at the stable. "You made the connection with Porado."

"Uh-huh. And his two pardners."

"They're tough. They were sent up for rustlin', which means they know cattle at least."

"I sure appreciate it, you sendin' them to me."

"You and Coco got a bad break here," said the marshal. "Anything else I could do?"

"There'll be a couple trunks from New Orleans," Buchanan said. "Maybe you could store 'em some place for us?"

"Haussling's all right. I'll take care of it and you can pick 'em up right here."

Buchanan sighed. "When Coco sees fancy duds he plunges right on. I got a few of my own things in one of them trunks. The soft life—it ain't right for a man."

"You goin' up the trail with Demetrius after your hide, and you won't be soft for long," said Doud. "Watch your scalp, too, Tom. The Comanches are raidin' and their cousins the Kiowas are up the Western Trail."

"The Western," nodded Buchanan. "And that's the way I figure to travel."

"Keep your powder dry, as my grandpa used to say."

They shook hands and Buchanan went to get Nightshade. The horse had been groomed and fed and the German was pleased, rubbing his hands at Buchanan's compliment, agreeing to store the incoming baggage against the return from Dodge City.

Buchanan snapped his fingers. "And down at Kak Johnstone's is some stuff belongin' to Miz Lu Lacy. Pick it up and hold it, too, will you?" He handed the man a silver coin.

Haussling's mouth turned down. "My vife, she no let me go to Johnstone's. Too many ladies with no clothes."

Buchanan said, "Then send your wife. Lu might need those things some day—if we live."

He mounted Nightshade. The big black horse was a bit sluggish after the mess of oats he had downed. They crossed a bridge over the Trinity River, the stream that meandered through Fort Worth as though designed for that purpose only. His thoughts ran to the Western Trail, which he knew fairly well, but not so well as he had known the Chisholm in the days of Abilene and in the days of the man known as Wild Bill Hickok, a nervous fast gun, now dead and buried. Wild Bill, shot from behind, gone with a gun wound, of course. Coco was right in his way, the short gun led to reckless murders. Buchanan carried his Colt's only when danger was imminent.

But now he loosened the rifle in its scabbard at his knee. As he headed for the plain where the cattle were gathered, his thoughts ran ahead. The situation was not good. There were dozens of details to be checked, bills of sale for the cattle in case of questions en route, checking the stores to be certain of food for the men, judging the horses in the cavva-yard and assigning the men their mounts.

And the men—Texas Kid and Coco, Porado, his two followers, Buchanan—and the cook, Lu Lacy. The herd was comparatively small, seven hundred and fifty or so, but men were needed to ride point, swing and drag, there had to be a night herder or two taking turns on duty, and there should be a wrangler, a boy to watch the cavvy and fetch and carry for the herders.

Someone would have to double in brass, as he had heard said in marching bands. He and Coco would be far better off in Frisco or Denver or Cheyenne or any other place watching a marching band, he thought—or even walking in it, much as he detested any notion of going afoot. He was marshaling thoughts along that line when Nightshade roused from his quietude, lifted his head and cocked an ear.

The bridge was barely behind them and the lights of the city still threw a small glow on the flatland. There was a shack of some kind off to the right. Nightshade snorted at it and broke into a gallop.

Buchanan snatched the rifle from the boot. There was the familiar song of the bullet, and a leaden bee buzzed past his head. The black horse had saved him by moving fast, he realized.

He bent low, a difficult task for a man his size, and returned the fire. Figures ran along a line reaching toward his destination. He led one with a long, chancy shot and heard a howl of pain. The other figures dropped to earth like mannequin targets in a shooting gallery.

Nevertheless, he turned Nightshade away. They deserted the trail, circled and came back.

The shack was pitch dark, throwing a small shadow. Buchanan rode in close, dismounted and prowled the perimeter of the place, rifle cradled under his arm. He heard nothing.

He moved in, suddenly kicked the door open. There was a low moan of pain and fear. He said, "Don't move, or you'll get hurt some more."

He reached into his vest pocket and found a wax taper. He ignited it, holding his rifle ready and the match on high. A man lay propped in a corner. He was bleeding.

Buchanan said, "Ran out on you, did they?"

"The dirty bastards. Demetrius took 'em away. I heard him." The man groaned again, holding his left arm with his right hand. "He said to hell with me. He don't even know my name, the sonofabitch."

Buchanan had spotted a bit of candle on a shelf. He lit it and bent over the fallen man. The wound was in his shoulder and it could be a bad one if left unattended. Men died of flesh wounds every day on the frontier.

Buchanan said, "I got some knowledge of wounds. Had a few in my own carcass. Hold still there."

He went out and rummaged in his saddlebags. He returned with clean bandages, an ointment, and some alcohol.

The man said, "You'd do this after I bushwhacked you?"

"Didn't get me, did you?" Buchanan began his task. This was a nondescript man, the kind to be found in bars like Johnstone's, ready for any job that would give him a small stake for gambling and a few drinks of rotgut. "You people are real interested in killin' me, now, ain't you?"

"It's the gal. Ow—that hurts."

"Uh-huh," said Buchanan. "If it didn't, you'd be ready for the undertaker. . . . The gal? You mean Lu Lacy?"

"She wouldn't pay attention to Demetrius. You know? She give him the back of her hand."

"After he sold her the cattle, that is?"

"Before and after."

"Oh. I see." That explained sending Skagg and the others to her. Demetrius meant to punish her in every possible fashion. It was a nasty thought.

"You got a name?" Buchanan finished cleansing the wound, applying the remedy he had gotten from a Crow Indian girl in Wyoming.

"Tuscon, they call me."

"Who do you know in Tuscon?"

"Why—nobody much. I mean, it's just a name."

Buchanan said, "Okay, Tucson. You got to see Demetrius again, right?"

"Not if I can help it. Not unless I got a bead on the bastard."

"Then send him a message. Tell him to keep comin' after Lu Lacy. Tell him Buchanan will be there to greet him."

The man called Tucson said, "I'll get the message to him."

"You be sure and do that. Big as this country is, paths keep crossin'. You ever notice that?"

"Too many times," said Tucson.

"Hope ours don't. It might be worse next time," Buchanan said. He finished with the bandage. The man got to his feet, and ran a hand over his sweaty face. He shook his head.

"I heard about you, Buchanan. I didn't believe it. Now I know it's true." He produced a .45 with astonishing quickness. The gun had been in his belt, and it must have been uncomfortable lying on it. "I can get to town safe enough. I'll see Demetrius gets the news. Let him sweat some. But look out, Buchanan. He's one plenty bad *hombre*, believe me."

"He left you here to die. Proves what he is," Buchanan said. "You take it easy now, don't start it bleedin' again."

"I'll spend the night right here," Tucson said. "In the mornin' I will make it back to town. Thank 'ee, Buchanan. I won't forget."

"Uh-huh." Buchanan went back and climbed aboard the rimfire, double-rigged saddle which was his home for so much of the time. Tucson might not forget, but he

31

wouldn't do a damn thing about it. Maybe he'd get word to Demetrius and maybe he wouldn't. Men like Tucson never were anything, never would be anything. They were the dregs of the West, and men like the Greek used them and deserted them at will.

It wasn't anything to waste time on. His problem was to work out the logistics of getting a herd of cattle up the trail to Dodge City with fewer men than needed and with a woman as cook. That was trouble enough.

Not to mention the frame of mind Coco would be in when he learned all the facts. Coco was a good friend, but he had his moods. When he was in one of them, he wanted more than anything to engage Buchanan in fisticuffs.

Once, long ago, Buchanan had manhandled Coco. The black prizefighter had never forgotten being thrown through a window in El Paso even though it had led to their escape from a rough situation. Since then he had challenged Buchanan to a fight a thousand times.

Buchanan always had an alibi. Either he was newly wounded, a most ordinary circumstance—or Coco was hurt in some way which did not permit hand-to-hand conflict.

Buchanan wanted to keep it that way It was best for both, he figured, that they never know who would win. He chuckled to Nightshade and rode toward the encampment of Lu Lacy—and now, Porado and his men.

THREE

BUCHANAN AWAKENED, staring upward. There were no stars in the pre-dawn sky. Instead he saw the tarred bottom of the waterproof chuck wagon. It had begun to rain at midnight. His boots were beside him, topped by his hat. A pool of water threatened them as the downpour continued.

He grabbed the boots and donned them, perched his hat on his red head, gathered the poncho around him as he made up his sougan and covered it with a tarpaulin designed for that purpose. He crawled out and put the bedroll into the chuck wagon for safekeeping at the moment.

Porado stood nearby, palming a brown paper cigaret. "Not a good morning, is it?"

"The herd will stand in it," Buchanan said. "No thunder or lightin' to scare 'em."

Porado said, "Am I to understand you do not sleep in the tent, then?"

Buchanan looked toward the dry, warm tent, wherein Lu had spent the night alone. "That's the way she blows."

Porado nodded. "It's good to know these things when there's a woman on a drive."

"Right," Buchanan agreed. "However, let's you and me go wake her up and get arrangements all set."

Coco Bean and Texas Kid straggled from beneath Porado's wagon where they had sought shelter. Dude Healy and Dutch Charlie were riding the watch.

Coco wailed, "I don't like this nohow. Even before we get to start, it rains down on us. This don't make no kind of sense to me."

Buchanan asked, "How much money you got, Coco?"

"I got two gold pieces. I could take them and get to some place where they are sports enough to set up a bout."

"Not from here, you can't," Buchanan told him. "Not even if you sell that Champion horse."

"I ain't talkin' about sellin' Champion," retorted Coco. He was very fond of the big roan. "That animal knows more about them cows than I'll ever know."

"You just come up the trail with us and you'll learn all there is to know about it," said Buchanan soothingly. "Meantime, who's gettin' breakfast around here?"

Behind him Lu Lacy said, "Just gettin' to it, boss, sir. Got to admit I overslept a bit. It's 'most four o'clock."

"You got fry chips?"

"Chips and shavins', your honor," she said meekly. "Have a fire goin' in no time at all, please, sir."

Porado smiled for the first time since Buchanan had met him. His lined face looked younger, brighter, less weary. "Show me where everything is, Miss Lulu. I'll be proud to help this first morning."

"And only the first morning," Buchanan added without rancor but with emphasis. "We're shorthanded, as you all got to realize. It ain't a big herd but I note long-legged critters and a few shes which will undoubtedly calve along the way. We got to lay down a set of rules and each and every one of us got to live up to 'em."

Porado said, "You will act as head drover?"

"I don't own a head of 'em," Buchanan said. "I just want to seen Lu get her bunch up to Dodge. If you got any notions, I'll sure be glad to hear 'em."

Porado said with dignity, "My small bunch is thrown in with hers. I will be glad to act as *segundo*. It's a small stake but it's all we own, my men and me. And we have the same enemies, you, Miss Lu and I."

"And they'll be lookin' for us," Buchanan said. "Okay, let's eat and talk and bring in Dutch Charlie and Healy and get everything straight."

"Right," said Porado. He was already at the heavy tail-gate of the chuck wagon. Texas Kid helped to flatten it, displaying all the appliances for trail drive cooking. Lu wore a loose wool cape, a rumpled felt hat, loose fitting Levi's and boots with high, riding heels. She plunged immediately into the task of getting coffee ready in the huge pot, as Porado skillfully built a fire.

Buchanan went to where the cavvy was roped loosely into a pack. Nightshade whinnied disgustedly, not too happy with his companion steeds. Buchanan counted heads.

There were fifty-two head. There should have been seventy, ten for each rider. Lu would be driving the chuck wagon and there should be yet another person to drive the supply wagon which Porado had contributed. They would be desperately shorthanded.

Furthermore, even with these few, the payroll would be one hundred and eighty per month, plus a hundred for Buchanan as head drover. Neither Lu nor Porado would have that kind of money, it was certain. Therefore, even if an extra man turned up, there would be nothing with which to pay him. He felt inside his shirt, touching the money belt wound around his waist. There was a stake in there, as always. He grinned to himself, saddling Nightshade, getting ready to ride around the herd as the dark sky lightened and the rain diminished.

"A day late and a dollar short," he said to himself. "A woman on the trail and jailbirds as pardners. What am I doin' in this mess?"

There was no answer. He rode around the edge of the sleeping herd. There were, as he had noted, a good many long-legged descendants of the old longhorns, but there were other breeds mixed in, especially among those Porado had brought from below the border. There was a big steer with a white blaze on his nose, looking up as Buchanan rode by, making a lowing sound.

Nightshade waltzed a few steps but Buchanan turned him around. "Damn if that ain't old Tom Fool," he said. "Now that's the first piece o' luck I've seen."

Suddenly startled the steer began to run awkwardly in the half-light. Alertly, Buchanan touched Nightshade and they followed, then broke ahead. There was the sound of drumming feet, horse and cattle.

It was a short chase. The light became better and the thief could be easily distinguished. He was trying to drive two fat steers southward. He was mounted on a pony that wore a hackamore and a folded blanket, no more.

Buchanan loosed a shot over the head of the rustler. The rider bent low and kicked at his pony. He rode for his life, deserting the steers. Old Tom Fool, clumping along, took charge of them. He was a well-known creature, and how he come to be in Lu Lacy's herd was something Buchanan would like to know. The biggest owners welcomed a lead steer, paid good money for one.

The fleeing pony put a foot in the hole of a prairie dog. It went down and the rider fell head-over-heels, rolling and trying to get to his feet to run. Nightshade lengthened his stride, enjoying the chase.

Buchanan rode alongside the would-be thief. He reached down with one hand. He caught the flying figure by the back of his buckskin shirt and lifted.

He had an instant handful of fighting, small Indian. Moccasins kicked out, fists flailed. Buchanan had to shake very hard to stop the furious attack. When his victim was quite out of breath, Buchanan dropped from the saddle and held him at arm's length.

The black, opaque Apache eyes were unmistakable. The boy could not be over fifteen. He was small, even for one of his tribe. He was dark-skinned and black-haired, a full-blood.

Buchanan said, "You speak English?"

The sullen face did not change expression.

Buchanan said, "Reckon you're hungry. Best you should come in with me."

"No!" The word burst from the boy.

"Not to jail," Buchanan told him. "To breakfast."

"You lie! Damn paleface lie!"

Buchanan said patiently, "A heap of palefaces have told a heap of lies to a heap of Indians. ¿Sabe? I know that. You know that. So let's you and me go in and have breakfast and talk it over."

"No!"

Buchanan said, "You can yell, but you're comin' in. I can hog-tie you and carry you or I can tie you to your pony and drive you. Or you can ride in ahead of me. Take your pick, young fella."

The Indian made a sudden move with his right hand, and produced a small, sharp knife, used for skinning animals. Buchanan thrust him away so that he stumbled and fell back upon his haunches. He crouched there like a dangerous animal.

Buchanan said, "Okay, mi hombre." He reached back and took the reata from his saddle. He moved very quickly; his speed always surprised those who did not know him. He made one quick cast and the loop encircled the Indian boy, pinning his arms at his sides. Buchanan spoke in Spanish, a language known to Apaches through their many raids into Mexico for loot and slaves. "The knife. Drop it."

There was a moment's hesitation. Buchanan jerked on the rope. The Indian came to his feet, staggered. He dropped the knife. Buchanan walked around him once, making a loop, then retrieved the weapon. Going close, he found the sheath attached to the back of the leather belt of the Apache. He restored the knife to its place.

He said, "You will mount your horse. You will ride ahead of me. You will do this because I tell you to. Do you understand?"

The youth made no reply. But when his pony came wandering near he leaped into the air, bound as he was, and landed astride.

"Very nice," Buchanan said. "I think you'll do to take along."

The young Apache rode head high, arms encircled, all the way back to the chuck wagon. Texas Kid and Coco were eating breakfast with Porado and Lu Lacy. The others were riding herd in the mounting sunlight.

Texas Kid said without surprise, "I see you got Lousy Luis. He tryin' to steal a head or two?"

Buchanan loosened the rope and the little Apache landed on his feet, staring straight at the towering Texas Kid.

"He was tryin'," Buchanan said. "What do you know about him?"

"Always stealin'," Texas Kid said promptly. "That pony, he stole that offen a Mex trail man. Nobody knows where he came from or nothin'."

Buchanan grinned. "Just like some others we know."

"I ain't no thief," said Texas Kid, flushing.

The Apache suddenly went into motion. He flew several feet off the ground. He had his knife in his hand again. He was aiming straight for the throat of Texas Kid.

Buchanan reached out. He batted the Indian down as though slapping a fly. He put one big hand on him and removed the sharp knife, balancing it, shaking his head.

"We could hang him. He was makin' off with the steers," he said. "He tries to kill people."

"Hang him? He's only a boy," cried Lu Lacy.

"He acts like a man," Buchanan replied. "A real bad man. I do believe he's hungry, too."

She said, "Then feed him. And Kid, you stop callin' him a thief."

Buchanan was watching Porado. "What do you say?"

Porado spoke softly, "I've been in jail. Charged with stealing cattle. One way or the other, I wouldn't see him hanged."

"Aw, I didn't mean that, neither," Texas Kid added quickly. "It was you said that, Buchanan."

Buchanan turned back to the Apache. He was weighing the knife in his palm. "You better eat. Then you better make up your mind. I'll give you 'till we move out."

Porado said, "We could use a boy."

"We plumb need one to drive the wagon," Buchanan said. The Apache known as Luis could understand him, he knew. He had been among them enough to read their infinitesimal changes in expression.

Lu had loaded a tin plate with bacon, beans and three of the fresh eggs she had been able to acquire. She motioned to the Apache. He stood a long minute, staring at Buchanan, ignoring the others.

Then he spoke in Spanish. "You would have me go on the journey with you?"

"Yes," said Buchanan.

Porado interposed, also speaking Spanish. "If you go along you will not be punished. You will eat. And we will see that you get back to the tribe after we reach Dodge."

"Mescalero," said Luis. "It is a long way."

"Were you a captive?" Buchanan asked.

"The Mexicanos, they caught me. They could not hold me," said the boy proudly.

They were forever raiding each other, the Mexicans and the Apaches. Who had begun it was lost in the mysteries of time. Each took captives and held them as slaves.

Buchanan said, "*Señor* Porado tells you the truth. We need another man."

Luis said, "I will go." Only then did he accept the platter of food. He walked away from them stiff-legged, carrying it. Texas Kid made as if to follow, but Buchanan prevented him.

"He's starvin'," he said. "Leave him alone. He don't want you to see him wolf it down. Lu—you'll have to give him more later on. Sorta force it on him, you know?"

"I know. I've been hungry," she told him.

"Ain't we all?" Buchanan looked at Porado. "I liked the way you talked to the Indian boy. Shall we get this herd started up the trail?"

"Any time you're ready," said Porado.

"We're short of everything. Even with the boy we're shorthanded," Buchanan said.

"I know."

"Then there's Demetrius."

"Of course."

"Well, sorta makes it worth tryin'," Buchanan said. He looked at Coco, who had remained silent and aloof and unhappy. "It'll do you good, friend. A new experience."

"Next to guns, I don't like cows," said Coco. "Nor sleepin' on the ground. Nor scoffin' the kinds of food that goes along with it all."

"Grub," Buchanan said. "On the trail it's just plain grub. You'll get used to it. By the time we get to Dodge, you'll be in the best shape you ever was in your life. I told you Luke Short's in Dodge. He's the promoter. I'll send him a telegram, maybe he can whup up a bout for you."

"I can get a bout in San Francisco and sleep in beds," Coco said.

"Well, if you truly don't want to go . . ."

"I don't want to go. I got no reason to go. I hate the idea of goin'." Coco waved his long, muscular arms. "But can I leave you alone with all these critters and these strange people?" He drew a deep breath. "And that lady? No, sir!"

"Thanks," Buchanan said. "You'll be a big help."

It was a motley crew. He ate the food Lu handed him and sat apart, turning it all over in his mind. It would take all of today, perhaps tomorrow, to get properly organized. Watches would be apportioned. Pairings would be difficult, since so few had trail experience. Lu might or might not be able to handle the team hauling the heavy chuck wagon. There were a thousand details that needed attention.

"Critters, strange people—and a lady," Coco had said. For once Buchanan heartily agreed.

The huge herd owned by Derick Demetrius was headed for Fort Griffin. He rode in a specially built carriage with extra springs that undulated gently across the plain. The soft cushions supported his heavy frame with ease and gave him the comfort he demanded.

He had been born in Boston, son of a Greek immigrant who made money importing olive oil. He had attended Harvard where he had not been accepted—he had been caught cheating at cards, dallying with a serving girl, and consorting with low and vulgar persons, including sailors. His father had turned him out and he had taken a vessel to California. Inside of five years he had made a small fortune in mining.

When the mines played out, he moved around the western frontier. He seemed always to be seeking a land into which he could fit his carcass and his personality. He had bought the services of lesser men upon numerous occasions and it had given him no satisfaction. He had rented women by the dozen but had found none for sale, not quite.

He had gotten into the cattle business in order to vie with pioneers such as Goodnight and Pierce. He had made money, but had gained no respect from the men he wanted to call his peers. There was something lacking in him, and the absence of it drove him to greater and greater depths.

Now he hired men like Bull Skagg to do his dirty work. He nursed great grudges against simple people like Lulu Lacy. He could engender instant hatred for a Tom Buchanan. Porado had refused to join his cattle drive and accept some responsibility in controlling Skagg and his men so he wanted to get even with the ex-convict. A coward named Boot Campbell drove his carriage and suffered every indignity because Demetrius knew enough to send him to prison. He owned the cattle and the cavvy and the men who worked for him. And he was thoroughly unhappy.

Campbell was a cross-eyed, wrinkled man of middle age. He sat hunched on the front seat, the reins in his hands. The team was a splendid matched pair of dapple grays. Behind stretched the herd, moving rather swiftly as the experienced herders drove them along under the direction of Beau Spandau.

The acquisition of Spandau, the elegant half-breed and superb cattleman who affected the *vaquero* style of dress, was a triumph. Demetrius had discovered his weakness, namely women. He had then arranged an involvement with a woman who was apparently married to a gunslinger. He had "rescued" Spandau and earned his gratitude—and paid off the prostitute and the gunman in the dark.

Spandau had recruited the score of drovers which formed the crew. They were all hard-bitten cases. Demetrius had insisted and Spandau had easily found the desired ruffians. The cattle business was filled with them, impatient men corrupted by the trail towns and their enormous appetites. They could not get work with decent outfits and were fair game for Demetrius and his foreman.

He was not so proud of Bull Skagg and his trio of cutthroats. They had already failed with Lu Lacy, and had been twice humiliated by the man Buchanan.

He paused in his thoughts to grit his teeth at the memory of Buchanan and the humiliation in Johnstone's. He would buy out Johnstone when he returned to Fort Worth, he had decided. And when Buchanan entered he would be shot down in his tracks, accused of something, anything which would excuse the killing. It was a warm, nice picture to conjure.

He returned to Skagg, who rode behind with Morgan, Krause and Gotch. There would be use for them. They were not true cattlemen, but he would work them—and bully them. He called for Skagg now, and the man rode up beside the carriage.

"Skagg, they tell me you're not a coward," Demetrius said loud enough for Campbell and the riders to hear.

Skagg turned dark red. "People don't call me that."

"But this Buchanan handled you like a baby."

"He took me by su'prise."

"You and your friends? All four of you?"

"There's a nigger sonofabitch and that damn big Texas Kid. And the whore had a gun."

42

"And they took the knife away from Bowie, too?"

"He's got hisself another. He'll use it on Buchanan if I don't beat him to it."

"And the woman. What about the woman?"

Skagg spoke cautiously. "You wanted her, uh, handled."

"Yes. I still want her—handled."

"Well, if they follow us it can happen."

"I want to be present when it happens. And Porado. You haven't forgotten about Porado?"

"You want him killed?"

"Punished," said Demetrius. "Maybe we could use him. He's a cattleman."

Skagg said, "You can't use him, boss. You got to kill him and them like him."

"Very well. Kill him, then."

"And the nigger. We'll kill him, too. You want the cattle taken up north?"

"Of that we will speak later," said Demetrius. "Make plans now. Then consult with me. The woman and Buchanan and Porado will be a day behind us on the trail."

"I'll do like you say."

"I know you will, Skagg. Because you may not be a coward—but you're afraid of me."

For a moment Skagg did not respond. Then he said without emphasis, "If you say so, boss."

"I say so. And you will do as I tell you. No more, no less. Remember, you failed once. Twice will finish you. Do you understand?"

"Okay, boss." Skagg rowelled his horse so that it shot ahead, frightened and hurt.

Demetrius watched. He was pleased for the moment. The double-barrelled shotgun loaded with buck was close to his fingertips. Skagg knew all about it. Skagg was scared, all right, knowing that there would be no one to avenge his death, no one to tell how it had occurred. None of his trio of cohorts would dare to speak against Demetrius.

It was a good feeling, but the trouble was that it wore off very quickly because Skagg, after all, was a nonentity.

Demetrius puffed on a cigarillo which looked out of place in his round face. There was always something to spoil satisfaction with his world.

FOUR

BUCHANAN PICKED UP one end of the rolled, heavy canvas which had been the tent. Luis Apache and Lulu struggled with the other end. It was early morning but everyone was up and about and working. Porado came and helped and they got the canvas into the wagon and spread it evenly across its width.

Porado said, "I don't understand this too well, but you're the boss."

"Where would you think the lady might sleep?" Buchanan asked. "We load the wagon up front and leave a place for her blankets at the tailgate. Luis, you'll drive."

"I do not drive. I ride!"

"Right now you drive. Maybe later you ride." Buchanan stared hard at him.

The Indian went to the pile of supplies and began loading them onto the wagon. Porado pursed his lips, then lifted a shoulder and went for his horse.

The herd was already moving, Tom Fool in the lead, stalking, the witless cows following him, the steers strung out. The point riders swung around, straightening the line. Coco was on the drag astride Champion. The chuck wagon was nearby and Lulu, attired in her Levi's and wearing a floppy sombrero, stood at the wheel, gathering the reins.

"Glad to see the end of that damn tent," she said. "It was a nuisance. But you plumb wore me out sawin' up the pole for the fire and all. If breakfast wasn't real good, blame yourself."

"Breakfast was fine," he told her. "And you got to toughen up if you want to make the trail to Dodge."

"I don't wanta toughen up too much," she complained. "Damn it, Buchanan, don't you forget I'm a lady."

"A lady you ain't. A fine woman you are," he told her. He picked her up and lifted her to the high seat. She was not a thin person but he grinned, handling her without effort.

"You are the strongest man I ever did know," she said, flushing a little, busy with the reins. "Lemme get this team goin' and out of reach of the dust and dirt."

Porado swung his horse alongside and watched her go. "She handles them well," he said. "Kid Texas is okay, too. He can ride point with me and we'll put Dutch Charlie and Dude on the swing. Sorry about Coco."

"New man always rides drag. He should have help back there, but don't tell him. He can do twice as much as most men."

"His horse is a great one. But what about when he has to ride one from the cavvy?"

"He'll manage," Buchanan said with more confidence than he really felt. "Main thing is to keep the dumb cows from knowin' they are bein' herded. Tom Fool will hit a pretty good pace for the first couple of days. After that it's up to us."

"Yes. And they do become distracted too easily."

Buchanan eyed him. "You sure talk good, Porado. Like people I've knowed who went to college."

Porado looked away, his face hardening. "As I say, there's two ways of doing time. The best way is to try and learn. I was a good boy. They let me read books.

46

An Englishman taught me language. I'm not proud of it, you know."

"I won't mention it again," Buchanan told him. "Meant it good, you know."

"I know." Porado nodded, rode away, heading for the vanguard of the moving herd.

Buchanan looked after him, pondering. Men came in all sizes and shapes. Porado could be a terrific asset, or he could be trouble all the way.

He joined Luis Apache, helping him to load the supply wagon. The boy was unhappy.

"My pony, it is in the cavva-yards," he complained.

"We'll take care of him."

"No good," said the youth.

Buchanan nodded. "Nothin' around here has been good for you, has it, Looey-oh?"

"Looey-oh? You call me that?"

"Better'n Lousy Looey, ain't it? And you're always cryin' like, ain't you?"

Luis shifted his ground. "The white-haired boy must not ride my pony."

"His hair is yeller and you know his name," Buchanan pointed out.

"Keed Texas! Ha, that is no name."

"Neither is Apache Luis," said Buchanan in Spanish. "I do not ask your true name. It is not to be spoken. I respect that."

Luis straightened. "No Apache speaks the tribal name."

"But you do not tell me your other name. The one the people may call you."

Luis growled, his black eyes burning. He moved a box of dried prunes to the front of the wagon.

Buchanan said, "And as for the horse, you stole it in the first place. Now I don't want to worry about you and Texas Kid. I got enough on my mind, you hear?"

Luis Apache surveyed the wagon. It was loaded. The big canvas would encompass the width of the load, acting during the day as a tarp, during the night as a mattress for Lulu.

"You worry about squaw, too," he said. He was on the

seat, picking up the reins. "Squaw got no business on trail."

Buchanan strode to the front of the wagon. "You keep your mouth off the lady, understand? I know you damn Indians when it comes to women. Get it in your head, this lady owns most of the cattle on this drive. She's your boss!"

The boy wagged his head so vigorously that his shoulder-length hair whipped across his brown face. "No! Squaw is not boss! You are boss!"

"I work for her," Buchanan said. "Get it into your skull."

"Apache no work for woman! The Mexicanos could not hold me. You cannot hold me!" He raised his right hand. "I work for you. I stay because you are *muy hombre*. You savvy?"

He loosed the reins and the team started ahead. Buchanan held back, allowing him the last word much beloved by Indians, especially Apaches. He needed the young fellow, he understood his pride. Luis was one of the people who did not believe in anyone, but did believe they had rights to the entire southwest. They were brave—Buchanan had met every kind of Apache, but he had never met one who was cowardly.

He mounted Nightshade and swung back along the line of cattle. Longhorns clicked here and there, direct ancestors of the early Texas breed. The herd moved briskly, against its will, goaded by Dutch Charlie and Healy. At the tail end of the drive, Buchanan found Coco astride the roan.

"How you makin' it, cowboy?" he asked.

Coco glared. "Don't never call me no cowboy. I got no use for the job. Ridin' all day, gettin' to chase strays, kickin' the lazy ones ahead. Is that any kind of work for a man hates cows?"

"Steers," Buchanan said. "Some cows, but mainly steers."

"But no bulls. Y'all does away with the manhood of bulls. It's no kind of life," Coco insisted.

"Wait'll the prairie dries up after the rains," Buchanan

said. "It's great trainin' for you, Coco."

"I got my own trainin' ways. Hey, there!" A steer had begun to stray, followed by another, a longhorn. "Git back there, you!"

He was off, Champion taking him to the strategic position, chivvying the cattle into the line. Buchanan rode up the other side of the line of march. It was all coming back to him, the sounds and smells and motion of the trails when the cattle were moving north to Kansas. It was a hard journey, but it had rewards. He was a man for the outdoors and it would be weeks before he slept between sheets again, or had a roof over his head. He began to sing, off-key, not too loud:

Come along, boys, and listen to my tale;
I'll tell you of my troubles on the old Chisholm Trail . . .
Come a ti yi yippi, yippy ay, yippy ay . . .

He passed Porado, waved, and went ahead, serving as scout to make sure of the road condition. There was almost no graze; the herds gone before had eaten it down past the roots, but the cattle were fat. There would be water the first night, he knew. They could do without the grass, but they needed the water.

They would soon be at Fort Griffin, which he remembered well. It had been established in 1867 to drive out Comanches and Kiowas who resented the killing of their buffalo. White buffalo hunters were protected by the army, red ones slain when and where they were found.

Saloons and shanties had abounded in Fort Griffin country, bad men and wild women—and the filthy hide-hunters. Buchanan had seen it in its last days. Now that the buffalo were reduced to a pitiful few, the hunters had departed and the army had pulled out, and nothing was left of the former boomtown but a few crumbling buildings. Bat Masterson and his brother had been there and the Earps and Pat Garrett and Charlie Bent and Luke Short, the dapper little gambler who was Buchanan's friend and tutor.

He shrugged and sang:

> Oh, give me a jail where I can get bail,
> If under the shining sun;
> I'll wake with the dawn and chase the wild faun,
> I'll ride with my saddle and gun.

He had, he realized, a rotten singing voice. But at night the cattle would not mind as long as he kept it low and crooned to them. He grinned and rode out to scout the road to Fort Griffin.

As night they made camp, roping the cavvy into a makeshift corral, bedding the herd where there was little grass but plenty of water from the recent rains. They were not too far from the lights of Fort Griffin, but they were on the plain and the smell of the smoke from the fire was in the nostrils of Buchanan and he felt alive again. He was weary, as were all of the crew. They were new and raw and not attuned to the work. But they were started, they were on the Western Trail to Dodge City.

Lulu cooked very little that night. Buchanan found her at the tailgate of the wagon, having trouble with her boots. He gave her a hand and she groaned.

"Just holdin' the lines," she said. "Just settin' up there all the day long. It wears a body out."

"It'll get worse before it gets better," he assured her. "You got to remember, it's your cattle. It's your big chance."

"I remember, I remember. It's what keeps me settin' there with a sore behind," she told him. She turned toward the wagon and again he plucked her from the ground and sat her above him. He was laughing and she laughed with him.

"Now you can get to bed," he said.

"I aim to do just that." Her eyes were already closing. "I got to be first up to make the fire . . ." She wrapped herself in the blanket. "Oh me . . . Oh my . . ." Her voice trailed off.

Buchanan said, "Good night, Lu," and turned away.

Porado was a few paces away smoking a cigaret, looking at Lulu in her blanket, admiration plain upon his visage.

Buchanan said, "I told you she'd do to take along."

"Yes. I agree. She can laugh," said Porado wistfully. "It is good to be able to laugh."

"Best thing there is." Buchanan went to the fire. He was still hungry and there was a piece of meat and a biscuit hidden where he had cached it earlier. He reached for it. The package was gone from the chuck wagon. He grunted. His mouth had been all set for that sandwich.

Texas Kid said, "The damn Injun took it. I was too far away to stop him. He run into the cavvy."

"It's all right," Buchanan said. "He's probably real starved."

"Nobody's got a right to steal," said Texas Kid virtuously.

"Unless he's broke and hungry or one or the other," said Buchanan. "Don't you come high and mighty with me, young un."

Texas Kid hung his head and muttered. "Well, you know what I mean. He didn't have no right."

"If you two don't quit feudin', we'll see who's got rights to what around here," said Buchanan. He was angry at having been deprived of his snack and his voice was harsh. He moved on and found Coco stretched out on a blanket, face down.

Coco said, "Don't be askin' me what's wrong. Any horse but my Champion and it don't feel good where I sit, that's what. I don't like this cowboy business no better than I did. A lot less, if you want to know."

"I don't want to know," answered Buchanan. "It takes awhile to shake down. This crew we got, it might take longer."

"Dutch Charlie and Dude got the first watch," Coco said. "Then me and that Texas Kid. Then you and Porado. Is that right?"

"Right."

"What about the Indian kid?"

"He don't know it, but he gets up and starts the fire for Lu and does the runnin'."

51

"He ain't gonna like it."

"Nobody likes nothin' about this trip," Buchanan said. "People got to learn."

"I ain't never gonna learn."

"Sleep on it," Buchanan suggested. "Tomorrow's another day."

"But I got to get up in the night and nurse a bunch of dumb cows," Coco said.

Buchanan did not reply. He threw a saddle on one of the biggest of the horses from the cavvy. Nightshade was grazing, sniffing, resting against the next day.

A motley crew, thought Buchanan, riding out to check the night guard. Dutch Charlie and Dude Healy knew their business. They kept to themselves, seldom speaking even to Porado. They were riding silently around the herd now, expecting no trouble from the animals, watchful for human intruders.

Buchanan said to Dude, "Got to expect trouble with Demetrius just up ahead of us."

"Yeah."

"Don't reckon it'll come tonight—or real soon. T'other side of Fort Griffin, most likely."

"Yeah," said Dude Healy.

"Wake Coco or the Kid when the time comes."

"Yeah."

Buchanan rode off toward the other herder. He was himself a master of the noncommital when necessary, but the Dude could give him cards and spades and beat him at it. There was no way of judging him or Dutch Charlie. They were ex-convicts, and they had worked with and for Porado, that was all that was available.

He paused at the rope corral and unsaddled the horse. Nightshade was asleep. Buchanan's foot struck a recumbent form. He bent and recognized the Apache boy, wrapped in a single blanket. Nearby was the stolen pony.

Buchanan shouldered his saddle. His blankets were in the chuck wagon. He hesitated, wondering if Luis was really asleep. For a moment he thought of delivering a kick in payment for the stolen sandwich. Then he laughed silently at himself and went back to the chuck wagon and found his gear and made up his bed with the saddle for a pillow.

Then he rummaged around and found the remains of the side of beef they had slaughtered for the cook. He cut off a piece and went to the banked fire and fanned it. He waited grimly until the meat was broiled on the end of his stick, jammed it between halves of a biscuit and chewed determinedly. The result of his culinary effort was less than satisfactory.

From the rear of the supply wagon Lulu Lacy called softly but accusingly, "Buchanan? What you doin' fixin' your own grub?"

"Never you mind." He swallowed hard. "Get to sleep."

She replied, "I keep wakin' and hearin' things. And seein' things in the dark, too. The little fire looks so cheerful."

He banked it with care. "Never mind the little fire. Get your sleep, I tell you."

"Buchanan? Tom?" Sweetly forlorn.

"Sleep!"

"Talk to me awhile? Help me go to sleep?"

He heaved a deep sigh. He wiped his hands and went to the tailgate of the wagon. She lay wrapped to her chin and now her wide mouth smiled at him. He could barely make out the contours of her long body beneath the covers. He leaned an elbow on the wagon and spoke quietly, reassuring her. It was the final task in a long, long day of hard work.

But it was not the least pleasant job of the day.

They formed up over the days of travel. They began to understand the habits of each other, to work as a team. The herd moved quickly until the grass grew scarce. Buchanan, scouting ahead, saw nothing of the enemy from the camp of Demetrius but he did discover the need for emergency action. He came in at dusk one night when they were far short of Doan's Store, where they would stock up with supplies for the ensuing hard two hundred and fifty miles. Buchanan drank coffee as Porado's men and Coco put the herd to the scant graze. He said, "We'll have to swing off. There's nothin' ahead for two, three days."

"Westward?" asked Porado.

"It would be best. There may be Indians but there's a better chance of grass to the west."

"It'll slow us down a heap, won't it?" asked Lulu Lacy.

"Bound to. But you can't gaunt the cattle now. There's too much trail ahead, too many things to happen."

She said, "You know best, Tom. Lemme feed the animals and we'll talk about it."

Buchanan finished the coffee, rinsed his cup in the dishpan and walked apart with Porado. "Didn't see hide nor hair of anybody. It don't seem right they ain't hittin' us along in here."

"Demetrius is smart. He'll get us where he knows he's got the best chance," Porado said. "He won't risk anything."

"Mainly it's holes to the west. Not much runnin' water."

Porado said, "You think he's watching us that close?"

"I said I didn't see anybody. But I smelled some."

"Kiowa?"

"Kiowa, Comanche or Apache or all together."

"Then they may hit us any time?"

"I think you and me better double our watches. Seems like us two oughta know best when they'd move."

"Agreed," said Porado.

They separated and Buchanan walked to the cavvy. It was some time now since the Apache boy had taken it upon himself to double as horse wrangler. He was fussing over Nightshade, rubbing him down.

Buchanan said, "I think I had sign today."

"*Si, señor.*"

"You too?"

"They are out there."

"Your people?"

"That I do not know."

"Would it make a difference to you?"

Luis faced him. "They left me captive to the Mexicanos. What do you think?"

"I think you didn't go back to 'em when you could.

54

You hung around stealin' rather than go home. That's good enough for me."

"It is not good enough for the white hair boy. Nor the riders. Maybe *Señor* Coco. Maybe *Señorita.*"

"*Señorita?*"

Luis hung his head. "You are right. She is very good to me. She tries to know me."

"Uh-huh," said Buchanan. "Look, let Coco stand your early watch tonight. You and me, we'll wait until dark and then we'll make a little *pasear.*"

"Ah! That is good," said Luis, his eyes brightening. "You will let me borrow a gun?"

"Couldn't take you out there empty-handed." Buchanan went back to the chuck wagon. Coco wore a neckerchief now, a red bandanna, real cowboy style. He used it to cover his mouth and nostrils when the dust hit the drag in clouds. He scowled at Buchanan.

"You tell me this is good conditionin'? Man can't even breathe back yonder."

Buchanan said, "The night air is good. You can stand watch for Luis early on. That'll clear your lungs."

"Always doin' me favors, ain't you? I declare, I do believe you come on this here drive just to torment me."

Buchanan said, "And keep your eyes open tonight. If you shoot anybody, make sure it ain't one of us."

"I ain't goin' to shoot!"

Buchanan said, "If the Indians come, you got to do somethin' about it."

"I'll rip 'em with my bare hands," Coco declared. "I'll tear 'em limb from limb."

"You do that." Buchanan sighed. "I just hope one of 'em don't scalp you first."

Coco rubbed his close-cropped wooly head. "Injuns don't get this scalp. You leave 'em to me." He scowled, staring. "What you mean they comin' in tonight? Who told you?"

"Just a hunch. Watch for 'em, you hear me?"

"How come hunches are always for trouble?" demanded Coco. "How come hunches ain't sometimes for good?"

"You tell me," said Buchanan. He watched Coco shrug

and walk away. The prizefighter would be watchful, he would be ready with his fists, no question about that.

Lu Lacy moved around the rear of the chuck wagon. Buchanan said to her, "Like to borrow a gun."

"A gun? Short or long gun?" Then she blinked. "You don't need to borrow a gun."

"It's for Luis," he told her. "Couldn't ask one of the men. They're suspicious of him."

"Fact is," she said, "everybody around here is somewhat suspicious of everybody else. It's a strange bunch we got ourselves together here."

"The long gun. Keep the other one handy," he suggested.

"Yes. You can feel it. Uncomfortable, ain't it? All the men walkin' low."

"You can feel it." He admired her in the rough clothes. She managed always to look like a desirable woman. "Keep your ears open. You won't see 'em if they come. You won't hear 'em 'til they want you to."

"It's all new to me. I'm a town gal," she said.

"You'll learn. You're doin' fine so far." He accepted the rifle she pulled from the chuck wagon and padded away.

The tall form of Texas Kid loomed. "Hey. You goin' on a scout?"

"Might be. You know your watch? You got your sleep?"

"You takin' that lousy 'Pache with you?"

Buchanan heaved a deep breath for the sake of patience. "News does get around this camp."

"When you got a lyin', braggin' redskin it does. Whyn't you take me along?"

Buchanan stared at him. "It needs quiet out there. You got a big mouth."

"I can scout better'n any damn Injun. Besides, how do you know he ain't one of 'em?"

"He is one of 'em," said Buchanan. "Only he don't like 'em very much."

"You might think so. And you might be wrong," said

Texas Kid darkly. "You might just be the end of us all. I'll be watchin', you can bet."

"You do that." Buchanan moved on, checking the night camp, the cavvy, the herd gathered closer than usual. The Indian boy was waiting on the edge of things, squatting, looking at the sky. Dark, heavy clouds hinted that the rains were not gone for that season.

Buchanan said in Spanish, "It is a night to beware."

"*Si, señor.*" The eyes of the boy were on the rifle.

Buchanan proffered it, and he accepted it with reverence, turning it in his hands.

"We go," Buchanan said, handing over a small box of shells.

"The horses?"

"We walk."

Luis Apache nodded. Walking was something he knew about. He would always rather be on a horse, but like all mountain Indians, he knew the value of being afoot under certain circumstances. He followed Buchanan, taking three strides to the big man's two, but losing no ground as they went into the starless black night of the damp plain.

They were soon clear of the area of the camp. Buchanan slowed down. He felt oddly relieved to be out there alone with the Indian youth. He was always, first and last and in between, a man of peace, but a scout was a—scout.

Luis Apache ranged beside him. "They will be closer than one might think, *señor.*"

"Yes."

"There is a stink of them."

"Yes."

"But perhaps this is a scouting party?"

"Hope so."

"Should we part here?"

Buchanan said, "You go about a hundred paces to the north. Savvy?"

"One hundred. I know one hundred."

"Yes." He paused, not quite sure of his plan. Then he said, "I'll leave it to you."

"You leave it to me?"

57

"When you trust a man, Luis my boy, trust him all the way," Buchanan said. "Move easy and never mind signals. They'd know the bird calls and all that."

"Yes. They would know. God be with you, Buchanan." The Indian boy touched his arm. It was a rare gesture indeed.

Buchanan said, "With you, too, Luis."

He waited until he had counted off the hundred paces which Luis was taking, then he moved westerly. There were no stars to provide beacons but Buchanan—and Luis Apache—needed none, no more than they needed a compass. They could distinguish the points of the compass because they possessed the built-in knowledge of the plainsman.

The vibrations were straight ahead. Buchanan walked quickly now, a loping pace. There was danger in the night, but there was protection in the rifle which he carried in his hands, and in the six-shooter nestling in its holster. He had the advantage of knowing where he was, where the camp and the cattle were, where the attacking force must be. He stopped now and then to listen, straining his ears in the night.

He heard the metallic tinkle of a bridle almost directly ahead. He dropped to earth, easing the way with a bent left arm, holding the rifle in his right hand. Plains Indians for the most part eschewed other than rawhide bridles. There was probably a white man with this band.

Buchanan crawled on elbows and knees. He hoped Luis Apache might be doing the same, coming in from the north. After what seemed a mile of hard going, he paused, then flattened out. He squinted up at the sky. The clouds were thick and impenetrable. There was little wind to move them. He felt safe for the moment.

A voice came, speaking pidgin English, the voice of a white man. "You kill. You catch cattle. You make um big coup. Me pay in guns, bullets. You sabe?"

The response of the Indian was liquid, swift. It was neither Spanish nor Apache, one of the many tongues of the plains, Buchanan recognized. It gave full assent to the

58

suggestion of the white man. One of the men hired by Demetrius, Buchanan thought.

"Do it your own way," the white man suggested. "Any time. I got the gold right here. Guns and bullets later."

There was a grunt. Buchanan hitched forward. He would remember that hoarse voice. He could do nothing to intervene at this moment and he knew full well that the white man would be gone before the Indians started their raid.

He also knew the imminent danger to himself and to Luis Apache. Once the Indian ponies began to run there was no escape. He would like to know how many there were; he guessed not more than a dozen or fifteen. It was a time when all his senses were keyed to the utmost, when each second was sharply etched upon his mind. He was a peaceable man, but sometimes these moments seemed the most brilliant of his life.

He estimated that Luis Apache would be close enough to recognize the danger. There was no way two guns could prevent the raid. It was a moot question whether or not they would be able to survive without shooting. It depended upon the course taken by the raiders. If they veered right or left, one of them, Buchanan or the boy, would not live to see the ending of it all.

He moved away from the sounds, drifting noiseless like a cloud upon the land. The sound of the shod horse with the bridle faded, and he knew the white renegade had departed. He circled wider. He heard the leader of the Indian band give a guttural order. Soft hoofs began to pound upon the sodden, grassless surface of the prairie.

He read their direction. He flattened himself to the earth as best he could. Then he realized they were going the other way, in the direction of Luis Apache. He readied his rifle. If there was a single shot he would be forced to join in. He was committed to the Apache youth.

The ponies came on, heading for the camp and the herd. There was no other sound than that of their passing. He poised on the balls of his feet, ready to make the run and get on the rear of the raiding band with rifle and pistol. He took a deep breath—and heard his name called.

"¡*Hola*! Buchanan!"

It was a whisper, a croak from the throat. He ran to the north. A pony whinnied. He sped to the site of the sounds.

In the darkness Luis Apache clung to the head of a strong pony, gasping. Buchanan stumbled trying to reach them, went down on one knee. His hand met the face of a prone body, a dead body.

"Luis!"

"I . . . my knife . . . I dragged him down before he could run over me."

"You're hurt!"

The boy sighed. He said in Spanish, "*Sí*, Buchanan! I am killed. Take the pony . . . go . . ." He sagged.

Buchanan seized the braided rein. There was no time to ascertain the seriousness of Luis Apache's wound. There were lives to be saved, there was cattle to be protected. He would come back . . .

He said, "Where is it, Luis?"

"The heart. He stabbed me deep. Go, Buchanan. Go! The *señorita* . . . She was good to me . . . Go!"

Buchanan swung aboard the pony. There was only the blanket and the braided hackamore, but he knew how and he knew what must be done. He cried, "Hold on, Luis. I'll be back."

Then he was gone, bent close to the neck of the pony, talking in an ear, the rifle strung, his .45 in his belt, following on the heels of the Indian party.

He heard shots at last. He heard the cries of the Indians, high and frightening, cries intended to stampede the herd. He heard a steady drum of pistol shots and knew the raid had carried into the camp. He kicked the ribs of the pony and rode as hard as possible. The mustang staggered beneath his considerable weight. The sounds grew louder in the dark of the night.

They had penetrated the camp, Buchanan realized. The herd was stirring but it had not yet begun to run. The steady pistol fire meant that Lu and Porado and the others were fighting hard.

He swerved to circle the herd. No one was tending it; therefore, everyone was in camp. He rode to the edge of the action and made a flying dismount, digging in his heels, skidding to a stop.

There were three Indians whipping their horses toward the herd. He thought of Luis out on the prairie, bleeding, and aimed with care in the flickering of a sudden smidgin of firelight from the back of the chuck wagon.

He shot the three Indians off the backs of their ponies. He ran into the camp. His juices were boiling now as he wondered who might have been hurt: Coco, Lu, the Kid, Porado, the faithful herders. He held the rifle in his left hand and drew the Colt's.

Indians rode, shrieking, threatening, shooting, darting with their spears. He fired among them. They were circling now, trying at least to stampede the cattle.

Porado appeared through the smoke. He said calmly, "If there was more light we could pick them off. On the other hand if they could see us . . ."

Buchanan replied, "Kill if you must, but chase them southward. Luis is out there and if they find him . . . You know what they'll do."

"Amen," said Porado. He aimed and fired.

Now Indian ponies were kicking and running, riderless. Two of them bolted straight through the camp. Buchanan ran to the chuck wagon.

From beneath the hind end, Lu's voice came. "Buchanan? I think . . . I think I shot one. I think I did, honest."

"Shoot as many as you see," he said.

He moved on. Two Indians were riding down the lone figure of a man. Buchanan sprinted. Then he stopped, peering in the gloom.

The two braves were dragged off their horses. Their heads were knocking together with a great sound like the breaking of melons. Coco's voice rose. "You no account red people. Keep outa my way! I'll wear you out, blast your hides."

Buchanan said, "Under the wagon, Coco. Without a gun you'll get yourself killed."

"That's what they was tryin'," Coco said. "Aimin' right at me, they was. I don't like it under no wagon."

Another Indian rode in, yelling his death chant. Buchanan shot him before he could let fly an arrow at Coco. "I tell you, get your head down! This ain't a prize-fight!"

Coco ducked and there were yells from another part of the camp. Buchanan reloaded, running.

Porado called to him, "They're on the run. We did as you said. They're going south."

"Best light a fire and bury the dead," Buchanan said.

"They will all be dead," Porado assured him. "Dutch and Dude aren't gentle people, you know."

Texas Kid loomed in the darkness. Buchanan seized his arm.

"Catch up a pony. Better bring a shovel, in case."

"What you mean by that?"

Buchanan snapped, "Do as I say!"

The youth produced a short-handled spade as the camp-fire flamed and the scene was illuminated. The herd was milling and Porado was leading his men in calming the wilder steers, encircling them. Lu came from under the wagon.

Buchanan said, "Luis is out there. He's hurt. I've got to get to him. Watch over the camp, have some food ready. Men are hungry after a fight."

He mounted Nightshade. Texas Kid followed. Unerringly, Buchanan led the way. He had a dark lantern always in his gear. When he came close to where he had left the Apache boy, he rummaged for it, and lit it with a taper.

Luis Apache lay on his back, his arms outflung. One hand clutched the rifle he had not fired. A dead Kiowa in full war paint lay two yards from him. The sharp knife of Luis was in the Kiowa's chest.

Blood had begun to dry from the hole in Luis's body. On his face was a serene expression, a slight smile. Buchanan stared down at him by the light of the lantern.

"Texas Kid, you call yourself? Look at Luis Apache, who also has another name."

"Is he . . . is he dead?"

Buchanan was on one knee beside the prone boy. He put a finger on the pulse in Luis Apache's neck. He jumped up and reached for his saddlebags.

"Don't touch him. I got a salve here I can use. If we can tote him in . . ."

Texas Kid held the lantern. He said soberly, "I can figger it. He kilt the Kiowa and that's how you got the pony. We was gettin' it hot and heavy. Them three you shot—I seen it all—they were headin' straight for me and Lu and Coco at the chuck wagon."

"Hold that light steady." Buchanan found the wound. It was not quite in the heart, he saw. He emptied his canteen, cleansing it. He found the white, clean bandage he always carried. He applied the famous herbal mixture.

Texas Kid was talking in a low-keyed monotone. "Him and me, we didn't get along. I suspicioned him and he saved us, gettin' that horse for you."

"Never mind that now."

"He was left with the Mexicanos by his folks. Okay. I was left behind, too. My paw and maw and big brothers and sisters, they hadn't time for me. They left me behind in Louisianna. Took me ten years to get away. I been runnin' up and down and tryin' everything goin'. And I'm alive. Just barely, but I do know horses and some about cows. I ain't useless."

Buchanan said gently, "Like many another button on the run. It ain't anything to feel shamed about. It's what happens to lots of us."

"You, too?"

"I went up the trail when I was fifteen," Buchanan told him. "My folks were dead."

"And you were scared, too?"

"Everybody's scared now and then. But if you feel good about what you done, then that's enough. That's somethin' to stand on."

"I was scared tonight. But I didn't run," said the Kid.

63

He paused, then added, "Not as brave as him. He's like to die gettin' you a pony."

Buchanan said, "Help me lift him. Nightshade will walk easy. You watch out and be ready if anything goes wrong. Bring that rifle."

"I'm sorry for what I said about him."

"Forget it—until you can tell it to him," said Buchanan. He got into the saddle and held the Apache boy in his arms like a baby. Luis was amazingly slight. "Made of Indian rubber," Buchanan muttered and had to grin at the unintended pun. They rode for the encampment. There, the short-handled spade would be needed in the burying of the dead raiders.

FIVE

THE SUN came up early and the clouds vanished, but the stagnant odor of death was upon the camp. Buchanan sent the herd on ahead with Dutch and Dude and Porado, but the others remained to do the dirty work. Coco and Texas Kid dug a trench for the corpses. Buchanan butchered the dead and dying steers caught in the cross-fire of the previous night. Lulu Lacy attended Luis Apache.

They had rigged the canvas in the back of the wagon to make a sling for the wounded youth. Buchanan stripped him, washed him and attired him in an old nightshirt. Lu kept watch as fever mounted. The magic of the Crow Indian medication became apparent at dawn. The crisis passed.

Lu said, "It's hard to believe, ain't it?"

"Not when you've seen it," Buchanan assured her. "The Crows are in touch with nature. They know things we don't even dream about."

"Can we move Luis?"

"We'll move him. I need an hour of sleep. Wake me

and I'll get on up ahead and see what else they got fixed for us."

"Demetrius?"

"A white man with a hoarse voice," he told her.

"Boot Campbell. He sucks around all the time, a cockeyed, wrinkled old coot. Drives for Demetrius."

Buchanan said, "I'll keep him in mind."

"You'll need more'n an hour sleep."

"Two hours, then."

"It's too much," she said, sighing deeply. "Too much to ask. I can't even pay your wages."

He looked past her at the sleeping Indian boy, then turned to survey the scene, the ditch, the sweating Coco and Texas Kid. "You get tied in, Lu. You start somethin' and there you are. I'm a peaceable man but I'm into this and Demetrius is up ahead and there's a reckonin' to be made. So let me sleep."

He crawled under the wagon, adjusted his sougan and was unconscious within seconds. He could always sleep when sleep was needed.

But he seldom dreamed. Now, with the sun blazing down, he thought he detected seared grass, trees bending, brown with neglect, waterless holes where cattle lowed in agony, vague shapes of people staggering like lone prospectors on a desert of hot sand. He turned over once and groaned. Then his brain mercifully blacked out so that he could get the much needed rest.

It was almost noon and the sun was hotter than ever. Buchanan rode Nightshade out past the slowly moving herd. It was as if it had never rained on this plain. There was no grass for grazing, the mud had turned to dust within half a day. Nightshade whinnied once and Buchanan stopped to pour water from the canteen into his hat so that the big black animal could snuffle and moisten its throat. Then he remounted and ranged out, searching for the next water hole.

When he found it a coyote was hunkered down, drinking. There was very little left and the mud was already drying. The coyote slunk away at the sound of approaching strangers. Buchanan watched. There was enough of the fluid left to satisfy Nightshade and to refill the canteen, he hoped. He dismounted and began to loosen the bridle.

The coyote wailed, staggered. Buchanan whirled, staring.

It was over in a moment or two. The prairie wild dog stretched out stiff.

Buchanan knelt. He put a finger in the water, tasted. It was bitter, it had a high odor. Nightshade cocked an ear and Buchanan nodded, leading the horse away from the poisoned well.

"Man with a hoarse voice," he guessed. "On his way to the Indians—or on his way back to Demetrius. But he ain't the only one. It's the one who puts him up to it. Okay, here we go."

In the saddle again, he headed for the herd behind him. Kid Texas was driving the wagon now. Porado and his two were riding in the van, Coco was on the drag. The old steer Tom Fool was holding the cattle together at a leisurely pace, proving his value to the undermanned drive.

Buchanan said, "Skip the water hole comin' up."

"Poison?"

"Uh-huh. I suggest you angle westward."

"East or west, we'll need water."

"You got some little time before they begin to get skittish," Buchanan said. "There must be graze and water both if we can keep 'em together."

Porado said, "We'll keep them together."

"Tell Lu, will you?"

"I'll tell her." Porado hesitated, then added, "I take it back about bad luck. She's quite a lady."

"She is that," Buchanan agreed. He rode out. The sun grew hotter with the hour. It was too early for such heat; no one would be prepared for it. The herds up ahead would certainly drink up all the water not running in a riverbed. Under the circumstances, it was a long way to the Red River.

He saw another coyote running after a jackrabbit. There

67

were a few birds and an occasional buzzard in the sky. Otherwise the plain was vacant.

He had only gone a mile when he picked up the trail of a large herd of cattle. He knew at once that Demetrius had also been forced from the regular line of march toward Doan's Store on the Red. Porado would recognize the plain sign when he came to it; therefore, it was best to keep going. He set Nightshade on an ambling pace and went due west.

It was a long ride. For a while he despaired. Sage brush and sand, gnarled small trees in a lopsided grove near a tiny water hole, they all added to nothing of value. He slowed down, staring ahead as the day waned.

Then he saw a rise in the land, not quite an escarpment, but an elevation of a few feet. Heat waves blurred his vision. He pressed on. Suddenly there was green grass, not much of it, very coarse, but a graze. It was several miles off the trail; it would delay the progress of the herd but it would be a life saver.

Nightshade tossed his head, rattling the bridle. He whinnied and pranced a step or two. Buchanan gave him his head, not for the first time nor the hundredth. They went over a rise at a brisk pace.

The growth was greener. A mist rose in the sunshine and down from the hills beyond came the sound of rippling water. There was a creek and Nightshade made for it.

Man and horse drank. The water was cool and clear. Buchanan filled his hat, emptied it over his head. The sun was far hotter that it should be this early in the year. Everything seemed a bit freakish, he thought, and the fun had gone out of trail driving when death had entered in the night. Somewhere up ahead Demetrius plotted and planned and sat safely beyond reach.

Porado would follow his trail, Buchanan knew. He adjusted the cinch, replaced the bit in the mouth of the big black horse. He mounted and rode slowly northward, picking up the wide plain markings of the cattle owned by Demetrius.

The nooning of the drive was late because of the tardy

start. Porado sat on his heels at the chuck wagon and drank a second cup of coffee, watching Lu Lacy. She finished the stacking of the tin plates, already dipped in hot water by the men as they finished the meal. She wiped her hands on a rough apron made of a flour sack and reached for a large bottle. She carefully poured a milky liquid over her reddened hands and wrung them together.

Porado said softly, "Glycerin and rose water."

She smiled at him. "Not many men know 'bout it. Keeps the skin somewhat soft."

"I knew a lady once." He rinsed the coffee cup with care. He looked away from her. "Miss Lu."

"Yes?"

"You do a good job."

"Buchanan says we ain't seen anything yet."

"So. Buchanan is usually correct. We head westward, you know. We lose a day now, maybe two days. But we may fatten the beef by so doing."

"Whatever you men decide." She walked to the wagon and looked at Luis Apache. He apparently slept, shaded from the sun by a flap of canvas. "I just hope this one gets better. Texas Kid's wasted drivin' the wagon."

"Maybe we could hitch it up behind." He gestured at the chuck wagon. "If the horse would trail it might work."

She said, "I'd rather wait and see what Buchanan says."

He was silent for a moment, his face shaded by the brim of his sombrero so that she could not read his face. Then he said, "Yes. You're probably right."

She went toward the wagon seat. He stopped her once more.

"About the Duke and Dutch," he said looking straight at her. "I wouldn't want to see you alone with them."

"I keep my pistol handy."

"Even so."

She said, "Porado, I know men real good. I know what's into them. Them two, they're no different than a hundred others I've known. I'm no lily, you oughta know that."

He flushed darkly and said, "None of my business, of course. Just meant it friendly."

She called after his stiff back as he stalked away, "Hey,

69

it's okay. I mean, thanks a heap. I mean, I know you was thinkin' of me."

He gave no sign that he had heard her. She sighed, and wiped surplus glycerin and rose water on the hands and wrists of Luis Apache. She returned to the chuck wagon and clambered onto the high seat.

Coco rode up alongside as the herd began to trek north and west. He called, "You reckon these people know where Buchanan headed at?"

"They follow tracks," she said. "They know."

"They better had. This here trip ain't nothin' I'd put up with 'ceptin' for Tom."

"I appreciate it," she said. "I know that nobody loves me or my herd. So let's get on with it."

"Yes, ma'am," he said. He covered his mouth with his neckerchief and dropped back to ride drag all alone, a job he was learning to hate with a passion.

Texas Kid appeared. He had the cavvy trailing the herd. He was worried and anxious that it wouldn't work. He climbed up, took the reins and clucked to the horse. The wagon fell in alongside the clanking vehicle driven by Lu.

"Take 'em out," he croaked. "Hell of a note, drivin' a damn ambulance."

Nobody was happy, thought Lu. Nobody was sure of anything—when Buchanan was absent. She wished he would return to them. She hoped she had enough glycerin and rose water to last the trip.

Porado had been friendly for the first time just now. Kid Texas was remorseful in regard to Luis Apache. Coco was doggedly doing his menial job. Dutch and Duke were people she did not concern herself about. If Buchanan were safe, if he found graze and water, she would be content.

She had always worshipped Buchanan after her fashion. Her weakness for men with dimples in cheek or chin was something over which she had no control. None had in anyway resembled Tom Buchanan, that was for sure. She did not want to make that mistake again.

Buchanan was miles ahead. It was coming on twilight and he had been all day in the saddle. He had not pressed Nightshade, knowing the resources of the big black, but they had been a long while on the road. He found a small stream and unsaddled, removed the bridle and let the horse graze and drink the clear water.

That Demetrius had not come this far west of the trail was plain to see by the absence of track. He was forging ahead, utilizing whatever had been left by the earlier herds. Buchanan was curious to see Demetrius's drive and the people on it, especially one with a hoarse voice. It was a capital sin to incite Indians to attack a white group or any white party, under any conditions.

He stretched out on his back, hat tilted over his eyes. It was a peaceful time of day and he wished he were back in the high plain of New Mexico which he had learned to call home.

Now there was this job to do. Once accepted, it must go forward. No one realized the danger that lay ahead, he thought. He had assayed the man Demetrius and he well knew the character and capabilities of such as Bull Skagg and company. The Greek would have surrounded himself with gunfighters as well as drovers. If they made a sortie in force the few who drove the Lu Lacy-Porado cattle to Dodge would be wiped out within the hour.

It was times like this when his old scars began to itch, some indeed to pain him. He got to his feet and removed his upper clothing. He bathed himself in the cold water of the creek as the last vestige of reflected sun drooped below the western horizon. Yesterday it would have been cool at this hour, now it was humid. Typical Texas weather, he thought, entirely unpredictable. He put on his shirt and called to Nightshade. Stars came and twinkled at him as though there had never been a storm.

He saddled up and headed north. Porado could follow his trail so long as it was fresh, he knew. He was a day ahead of the slow progress of the herd. He thought he could easily catch up with the Demetrius drive tonight.

He was right. It was no more than ten o'clock when

he heard the riders singing their night songs to the cattle. He rode slowly, reading the sign by the few stars. The riders knew him no more than he knew them. He closed in, watching, picking out the biggest of them. He unlimbered his rope. He held it low, against the pommel, and began humming his own song, "The Streets of Laredo."

The biggest of the night herders came within reach, stopped, craning, asking, "That you, Leo?"

"Uh-huh," said Buchanan.

"Then git around the t'other side, dammit."

"Sure," Buchanan said. He whipped the reata in a short, sure straight line. He caught the herder around the shoulders and Nightshade responded to the knee and the man crashed to earth. Buchanan was on him in a trice, hogtying him, gagging him with his own kerchief. The man lay stunned, semiconscious.

Buchanan whispered in his ear, "Make a move or a sound and you'll be dead. There's people watchin' you."

He emptied the man's rifle and revolver and hurled them into the night. He climbed aboard Nightshade wearing the herder's hat, his own attached to his saddle—he was fond of the Stetson which he had bought new in El Paso not so long past.

Now he was riding the herd, humming his song, watchful, pausing every so often to listen. No one paid him any heed. He located the chuck wagon where it was situated, away from the herd, and he saw sleeping men in their blankets. He was puzzled by the luxurious carriage for only a moment, then perceived the guards stationed around it. The seat folded back to make a fine, soft bed for the boss man. Demetrius did himself well, Buchanan conceded.

Still there were ways and means. Buchanan dismounted, kept Nightshade close by and waited. Sooner or later the other night men would discover the one he had tied up. Each moment was now precious. He heard voices murmuring at the carriage, he made out a tiny night light of some sort. He crept closer, his revolver hitched convenient to his hand, the rifle ready in the boot upon his saddle. Nightshade was quiet as the shadows of the night.

Buchanan counted the sleeping men. There were four, and he could dimly make out the features of Bull Skagg among them. Another came jauntily toward the carriage which could now be seen sheltered by a tarpaulin. It was Beau Spandau, the boss herder, the top cattleman of the group. Buchanan could have shot him and put the Demetrius drive in trouble then and there.

He inched closer among the sleepers, crouched low and listened. Spandau reported all was well.

Demetrius said petulantly, "Nothing is well so long as that bitch and her stud Buchanan are behind us."

The remembered hoarse voice responded, "Geez, boss, I did all I could. There was plenty of them Injuns. They shoulda easy stampeded the herd and killed anyway a couple people."

"They didn't," Demetrius pointed out with violence. "Damn it, they didn't even get to the supplies."

"I did my best. That damn Buchanan, he pulled some kinda whizzer on 'em."

Spandau interposed. "That damn Buchanan is a cowman and a fighter. You want him killed you can send somebody else after him. My advice is to push on. We got the people, we got a deal to make in Dodge."

"I want that woman. I want Buchanan dead. Porado—he should be in the same grave. I want their cattle."

"It's branded," said Spandau without expression, his voice flat. "People in Dodge know."

"We could take it to Montana, fatten it, rebrand it," said Demetrius. "It's prime beef."

Spandau replied, "We got enough to do, gettin' this herd on. There's a drought comin'."

"You're crazy. A drought? Nonsense, we've had nothing but rain."

"The early sun," said Spandau. "Day like today—that spells drought for the country up ahead. Best we push on. Them people behind us will be in trouble enough."

"Then we'll hit them again," Demetrius said. "I want them, do you understand? I want them broken on the wheel."

Spandau said, "That's okay with me. But cattle are my

business. If you had the woman—another matter. Breakin'
women, horses and wild steers, that's my trade."

Demetrius said contemptuously, "Second-rate women,
those are your favorites. Let me sleep now. There's no
one to do what I want done."

Spandau came out into the night and breathed deeply.
Buchanan could have reached him in one jump. There had
still been no outcry from the herders on the night watch.

Buchanan felt the friendliness of the dark. Nightshade
moved without sound, following him as he held lightly to
the reins. They moved like huge ghosts within the camp.
There were a half dozen men sleeping here and there
including the cook. The chuck wagon was enormous and
there were two supply vehicles to keep Demetrius in the
style to which he was accustomed. No one seemed to
notice as they prowled. The hoarse voice, unforgettable,
sounded again.

"The damn Injuns just couldn't cut it, is all."

Demetrius snarled, "You could've gone in with them.
You could've tried to show them the way. You're not up
to that, are you, Campbell?"

"It wasn't my job," protested Campbell.

Buchanan trailed them from fifty feet away. The very
size of the camp gave him a certain freedom from detec-
tion, he realized. He might be any one of the herders—
so long as he bent his shoulders, concealing his height
and girth.

Demetrius said, "And you gave him half the money.
It's gone. You'll pay for that."

Campbell whined, "It wasn't my fault."

"Ah, get out. Go and sleep it off," Demetrius said
scornfully. "I should've sent Skagg and his men."

The man with the hoarse voice stumbled from the
carriage and its engulfing tarpaulin. Buchanan followed
him to the edge of the camp. Campbell was reaching
for his sougan when the alarm went off. They had found
the rider who had been wrapped up by Buchanan. There
were shouts and someone lit a lantern.

Buchanan took time to pounce. He lifted Campbell by
his shirt front. "A Scotsman, are you? I don't believe it."

He struck full-armed. Campbell caught the blow along-side the head. He flew ten feet, then went down and rolled over and over.

Nightshade was already running. Buchanan made a flying mount. He circled and came in near the slumbering cattle and drew his revolver. He fired in the ears of a couple of leaders. They raised a complaining sound and the night became filled with confusion.

Buchanan rode on. He raised his voice in an Indian war whoop, remembered from long ago. Someone yelled, "Injuns! Everybody turn out! Injuns!"

Buchanan now held his rifle ready. The herders were too busy to notice, he found. The herd was on its feet, gaining speed. It was running. Demetrius was screaming from his carriage. A stampede was under way.

Buchanan turned southward. He was satisfied. The man named Campbell would not eat without pain in his face for some time. The fat would be trimmed from the Demetrius cattle before Spandau got them quieted down. There were too many men on the drive. They could make war any time and finish off the Porado-Lu Lacy crew, including Buchanan—but if they did, they would suffer losses too great, he thought, to make it worth the chance.

He reloaded his Colt's and rode on. When he came to the camp, there was a slight figure leaning against the rear wheel of the chuck wagon. He unsaddled Nightshade and Lu squirmed out of a blanket and steadied herself against the hub of the big wheel and asked, "Where the hell you been? I was worried to pieces, there."

Buchanan said, "Been a bit busy. I see Porado brought y'all here to the water."

"Of course he did. He's like you. He just gets things done." Her tone was petulant, but she was bringing out a huge sandwich of bread and meat and a plate of cold beans.

"How's the boy?" asked Buchanan, reaching for the coffeepot which was always on the fire.

"The fever's gone, I think," she said.

"You been up all night lookin' after him?"

"Couldn't let him die, could I?" She wrapped the

blanket around her shoulders. "That salve you put on him sure is something wonderful."

"Indian cure for an Indian kid," Buchanan said. "Not that I haven't used it on myself."

"I got to get some sleep now, though," she said wearily. "It's damn near breakfast time."

Buchanan said, "Turn in. And . . . you're some kind of a lady, you know."

"Ha! A lady is one thing I ain't." She tossed her head, starting for the wagon beneath which she had folded another blanket.

"Lady is as lady does," Buchanan told her. "You'll do to cross the river with, Lu."

"Pah!" But she smiled widely as she huddled down to get a couple of hours sleep.

Buchanan ate. After a few moments Porado came and poured coffee, thick as molasses.

Buchanan said, "They're stayin' east of us. Not right on the trail, but just off it a bit. We're fifteen, twenty miles west of 'em."

"Best we stay here. There's a dry spell coming up."

"Right," said Buchanan. "Fill everything that'll hold a pint before we leave here. I didn't find runnin' water between here and Demetrius's drive. We can go a bit slow, let 'em get in and out of Doan's Crossing."

"How many men has he?"

"Twenty, maybe more," Buchanan said. "He's ready to fight a war. We ain't."

Porado was silent for a moment. Then he asked, "How close did you get?"

Buchanan told him. They sat together awhile over the fire, neither having much more to say, both of them thinking carefully over the immediate future.

Finally Buchanan proffered, "A day at a time. It's the only way."

Porado nodded. They went to their blankets.

SIX

THE DAYS went by, the sun hung in the burning sky, sometimes high, sometimes unseasonably hot. The cattle moved as the terrain dictated, no more than twenty miles per day when all was at peak, as little as ten when the going was rough. There was graze, but slowly it turned brown. They found no running water, all the streams had dried up. They had to make the Red River and they were behind schedule, Buchanan knew.

There were compensations. Luis Apache had regained his strength and was again driving the wagon and doubling on other occasions. Texas Kid seemed to have found some peace within himself and no longer bickered. A discipline had manifested itself. Everyone knew his or her job and because they were shorthanded, all turned to with a will.

At daybreak Buchanan was up and ready to ride. Lu Lacy had his breakfast ready, beans and biscuits and blackstrap with the usual black coffee for his tin cup. Porado came to them, a man who never seemed sleepbound even when suddenly awakened.

77

Buchanan said, "There's some hills up yonder. I'll be lookin' for water. You might make it an easy day, the critters ain't gettin' fat off the trail these times."

Porado said, "We lost two. But we picked up some strays."

"Just make sure they're mavericks," said Buchanan, grinning to remove any sting from the advice.

"I'm not saying Dutch or Dude wouldn't alter a brand," Porado replied, unsmiling. "But I know better than to let them do it."

"We don't need that kind of trouble."

Lu said, "We don't need any more trouble than we got. The water barrel's so low that pretty soon there won't be coffee. You know what that'll do to y'all."

Buchanan said, "I think we'll have Kid Texas drive the wagon today. I'll take Luis with me."

"Trouble?" asked Porado. "Indians?"

"Nope. It's just that sometimes two heads is better than one. Or two noses, maybe. Okay with you?"

"Certainly," said Porado. The sun was beginning to throw a rosy shine on the eastern horizon. He was looking at Lu as she hustled about the chore of getting breakfast. He did not take his eyes from her as Buchanan saddled up and mounted Nightshade.

Lu lifted her hand, turned her face, smiling, open, warmth exuding from her. "Take it easy, Tom," she called as he rode off to pick up the Apache boy and his favorite horse. "I'll have a plate for you when you get back."

Buchanan waved a hand and went on. He had noticed the preoccupation of Porado when Lu was around. He thought he knew what the man felt—he admired Lu as much as any woman he had ever known. She was a bright and courageous lady. Porado was an ex-convict, a man with half the number of cattle on the drive as those owned by Lulu. He was also a private man, reserved, probably afraid to show emotion lest he be knocked down again, hurt again. It was something to think upon as Buchanan rode out with Luis Apache happy at his side.

They rode miles at an even pace. The hills were bare,

the sun rose and shone in a cloudless sky. The sweat ran on them.

Suddenly Luis Apache stood in his stirrups. Buchanan reined in. Luis was pointing eastward. There was a small stand of Texas pine atop one of the hills.

Buchanan said, "Gotcha, Luis."

They rode in the direction of the trees. There was a gentle slope, a rising to the north and east. At long last there was the sweet sound of burbling water. Luis let out a whoop and started for the hillside.

Buchanan hollered, "No!"

A shot rang out. A lock flew from the shoulder length black hair of the Indian boy. He swerved and came in a circle then, crossing behind Buchanan. There was no cover, no place to hide.

Buchanan unlimbered the rifle. He lay low on the neck of Nightshade. He rode with Luis beside him, heading past the hill with the tempting stand of trees, aiming to get beyond rifle range before the enemy could bring either of them down.

He saw a figure standing, pointing a gun. He fired from beneath Nightshade's neck, Comanche-style. The man threw the rifle away from him, staggered and fell.

Luis again let loose with his throaty, high cry. They rode on until they had come to a safe place, where they could see the hill with nothing between them but the floor of the plain. They dismounted and stared at one another.

"Demetrius has been here. He must've come onto that hill from the east," he said. "He don't want us to have that water, does he?"

Luis Apache said, "I think we get that water." He was carrying Lulu's revolver in his belt.

"It won't be easy. Better ride back and tell Porado what's up."

"But we could mebbe try them? Please, *Señor* Buchanan?"

"Try them? Without cover? How you aim to get to them?"

Luis Apache begged, "Lemme try? Huh? I go back

79

toward the herd. But then I try?"

Buchanan said, "Afoot?"

Luis nodded.

"If anyone can do it, I'll bet on a 'Pache," Buchanan said. Something had to be done before the herd arrived. He thought it through. Luis was well-recovered from his wound, and openly pining for vengeance. If Nightshade were rested for a couple of hours and the kid got into trouble, there might be a chance for a charge up the hill. Everyone underestimated the speed with which the big, black horse could cover ground . . . On the other hand, if they caught the boy, they would kill him without a second thought.

Luis Apache said in his own language, "It is that I am already dead, *señor*. Except that you brought me back. It is necessary that I do this. It is my chance to regain my spirit."

"*Sí*. I understand," said Buchanan. "Go with God. When you get close enough, signal me with two shots, quick and together."

"There will be two dead *hombres* if I shoot twice." The boy rode off, pretending to backtrack, remaining out of range. Desultory shots came from the hilltop. There were at least three men there, Buchanan thought. They could easily come down and cut between Luis and himself and engage in a battle they might well win.

He waited, watchful, believing all the while that they would not do so. Hired gunmen, he had learned over his long years on the frontier, had no stomach for open fights, even when the odds were with them. They knew he had a rifle, they knew he was a good shot. They would remain on their hilltop and defend it from cover, feeling themselves safe. They certainly knew that the Lacy-Porado drive was undermanned. They hoped to deplete it even more, he supposed.

But Demetrius had not risked it all. Like the gun-slingers, he was not up to a pitched battle, one in which he might suffer damage beyond repair. He was not that kind of gambler. He preferred to leave behind a few killers from amongst his army on the chance that they could get Buchanan or some others and leave Lulu Lacy, Porado, and the cattle defenseless.

Buchanan sat on the ground, allowing Nightshade to graze on the brown furze. It was another case of waiting and he hated to wait. He found his old field glasses in the saddlebag and focused them on the hilltop. He counted at least three separate figures, none of which he recognized. He hoped Campbell was one of them.

The sun was mounting in the sky. His eyes blurred and he lowered the glasses and resumed his line of thought. Luis would come at them like a brown snake. If he had luck he might provide a surprise. If his number were up, he might be killed, in which case Buchanan might also die, since he would not leave the scene without a fight.

It had come down to this situation so many times in his life thus far that Buchanan did not fear the consequences. The sun was now somewhat in the eyes of the men on the hilltop. He again tried the glasses.

After a long moment he saw something moving at the foot of the hill. It might have been a coyote or another denizen of the prairie. He blinked and looked again.

It was Luis. He had removed all his clothing but a brown breech clout. He was wriggling and crawling and sliding on elbows and knees. His revolver was concealed beneath his brown body, lest it glint in the sun to betray him.

It was, Buchanan thought, impossible for him to gain the top of the hill without being seen. A diversion was necessary.

He mounted Nightshade. He edged in closer to the hill. He lifted his rifle, took careful aim. He was out of range and intended to stay there, but he knew something of the kind of men who would be on that hilltop. He fired two shots. The sound echoed over the intervening space. Luis held tight to a small outcropping of rock.

There was immediate response from the hill. Shots sounded, lead kicked up forty yards short of Buchanan's position.

He moved closer, risking a ricochet. He fired a few

81

more shots. They were returned with interest. A lot of ammunition was going to waste this late morning. The sun climbed higher and it was just about noontime.

Buchanan looked again through the glasses. Luis had vanished. Buchanan persisted, knowing the ability of the Apache to make himself invisible. Nothing moved, not a tendril of green growth, not a bit of brown brush.

The boy had slid around the hill. Buchanan's diversion had allowed him to make a sortie which might bring him behind the enemy while Buchanan engaged them at the front. It was as if they had discussed the plan and were now carrying it out, yet no word had passed between Buchanan and the Apache. Buchanan was motivated by long experience—the boy, because it was his birthright.

It was a dangerous plan. Buchanan moved in closer. The bullets began spitting into the ground nearer and nearer and Nightshade shied as one skipped by within a foot. Buchanan aimed high and sent three shots on a parabolic mission which carried to the top of the hill.

He hoped he had their full attention now. Everything depended on distracting them from Luis Apache. He wheeled Nightshade in a circle, riding like a plains Indian, edging a bit closer to the hill. It was not a very steep slope, he saw as he came closer and looked through the glasses. The top was fringed by brush which gave the riflemen concealment if not true defense. There was no way he could sneak in and take a quick aim because he could not definitely locate his targets. He did confirm his notion that there were three of them active. The fourth, who had taken Buchanan's bullet, was not now in evidence.

Time passed on swift wings. Buchanan's circling was making them nervous, he thought. He came in recklessly close, no longer looking through the glasses for Luis Apache, trying to get the time right in his head for the move he must make. He would be going into guns but he could not know how many.

He had a theory about the charge. It was based vaguely on the old military precept, that men afoot did not easily withstand cavalry. It had worked for Buchanan several times. Now he was not so sure, with the canting of the land ahead of him, and the riflemen on the hilltop, hidden from view.

There was a silence as he rode with care on the edge of rifle range. Nightshade snorted. The sun was very hot as it reached high noon.

Then there were two shots close together. They did not come from the barrels of rifles, they were revolver shots. Buchanan clapped heels to Nightshade, heading him for the the run up the side of the hill. He leaned low, his rifle in his right hand.

Bullets came close to him. Nightshade whinnied and charged with all his splendid might. They were halfway up the slope when Buchanan caught sight of a form. He fired from the hip, one-armed, one-handed. The figure vanished with a howl, a hoarse howl.

Nightshade gained the hilltop. There was no further firing. Luis Apache sat cross-legged, revolver in hand. There were four dead men scattered about. He was grinning.

"Two for each," he said merrily. "That is fair, no?"

"Fair enough," said Buchanan.

Luis pointed. "That one nearly got me. You shot him just in time."

Buchanan dismounted and went to the prone form. He turned the man over with his boot. He saw the bullet hole in the head. The jaw was swollen. He bent and searched the man's pockets. There was some silver, not much. There was a folded envelope addressed to "Sandy Campbell."

"Didn't think he had the guts," Buchanan mused. "Still, he had Scottish blood, villainous as it might be."

Luis Apache said, "The water is yonder. It is an underground stream. It is very cold and pure."

"They didn't poison it. They figured on poisinin' us," said Buchanan. "With lead."

Luis asked, "Should I go back now and guide the others?"

"Your pony down yonder?"

"Beneath a bush," said Luis. "My shirt and pants, also. I think I had better dress and go back, no?"

"I think you had better, yes," Buchanan said. "And I ain't goin' to bury these carcasses, neither. Send the Kid and Coco or Dutch and Dude on up ahead. I'll be scoutin' the rest of the day." He added, "You did good, Luis, real good."

When the Indian boy was gone he looked over the corpses. They were ordinary men. They had been cowboys or farmers—outdoor people of some kind. They had strayed on the byways and accepted high pay from such as Demetrius. Now they were dead in a sorry cause. He felt nothing for them. He turned Nightshade back down the hill and rode on northward.

The death of the men on the hilltop should have depressed him, he felt. The waste of human life on the frontier was one of the matters which gave him pause in his wanderings up and down. Basically, he was not a man of violence; he truly believed in live and let live.

It was the villainy of the man Campbell which turned him around, he decided. The man had set Indians upon a company of people minding their own business, meaning no harm to anyone.

On the other hand there was the one who had bought and paid for Campbell. His day was to come. It would be a bloody day, Buchanan knew. There was no profit in underestimating the Greek. He was a man of many tricks. He was in pursuit of some dream of his own. That his dream might be a nightmare to Buchanan did not matter. The end would be the same, total victory for one or the other.

He deliberately rode westward, going farther from the main trail, farther than Demetrius herd's trail, seeking to avoid the confrontation as long as possible. If they could cross the rivers and reach Dodge he would have accomplished his purpose—to see the herd through. Ordinarily, it would have been a small task. Now it was becoming a nightmare.

At nightfall the fires gleamed around the Demetrius

camp. Spandau came to where the Greek sat, enthroned in a folding chair.

"The Injun's back," he said.

"So?" Demetrius was eating a tender steak, sopping up gravy with a biscuit.

"It was a washout. They're all dead."

"Campbell, too?"

"Every man jack of 'em."

Demetrius swallowed coffee, reached for a peach pie. "Buchanan again?"

"Seems like."

Demetrius ate in silence for a few moments. "A man can't let himself be exercised," he explained finally. "A man has to keep his brains about him."

"Yep, that's right," said Spandau. "A man has to keep a crew together, too. That is, if he wants this herd to get through to Dodge."

"You think we should proceed at all speed."

"I do."

"You think there'll be a drought."

"Every cattleman along the trail believes that."

"We got to harrass them," Demetrius said firmly. "We can't let 'em get through in good condition. You understand?"

"I understand. I also know it's my job to get our bunch to market," Spandau said bluntly. "Can't keep on losin' men every few days. Skagg and them, now, they ain't worth much to me. Campbell won't be missed. But the rest of the herders, they're my men."

Demetrius swallowed the pie. "It's a wise man listens to the help he hired. If it's good help. You're boss of the herders. I listen to you."

"I can spare Skagg, like I say, him and his dudes. They can get themselves killed by Buchanan, it's okay by me."

"They are wary of Mr. Buchanan," said Demetrius dryly. "The next attempt will be planned. By me. But nobody but me. Meantime, do your job, Spandau."

"Right you are." The boss herder turned on his heel and walked away toward the campfire where the men hunkered down, eating, drinking coffee, swapping stories.

Demetrius lapsed into deep thought as he digested his huge meal.

"Money is power," he thought. "I've got the money and I'll spend it. The woman must be brought to her knees. She must be broken. Buchanan must die. Porado too—and whoever else is part of them, that miserable pack, that ragtag and bobtail little bunch of gnats. One way or the other, they must be finished."

He belched politely and went to his carriage to spend the night asleep on the gently swaying springs, sheltered by a buffalo robe, guarded by Skagg and his men, his mind still working as he drifted off.

Buchanan rode Nightshade along the bank of the Red River. The herd came on, Tom Fool leading. The current ran strong but the river was not raging, it was not deep. The early signs of drought were plain.

He could see Doan's store on the other bank, an old adobe building surrounded by small houses and of course, the saloons. He had to make sure no ambush was laid there. He signalled to Porado by waving his arm, and dismounted to await reinforcement.

The day was unseasonably hot, as usual with this trip. Buchanan sat in the sun, his eye upon the little settlement. It lay somnolent in the heat. There was no apparent danger. He was about to remount Nightshade and try the crossing when a man came out of the town and moved toward him. Buchanan eased the revolver in his belt and stood waiting.

The man called, "That you, Tom Buchanan?"

"It's me." He looked again. "Brownie?"

"Yep." He was stooped and white-bearded, a mountain man who had turned buffalo hunter and who was now one of a vanishing breed. An arm was in a sling and there was a bruise under an eye. In his belt was a Bowie, seventeen inches long.

"Waugh," said Buchanan. "Heap trouble, no?"

"Demetrius. Man named Skagg. And some others. Hadda run 'em off with this." He touched the Bowie. "They got all the stores, though."

"Stores? You mean supplies?"

"Waugh. I mean vittles, every damn thing. Demetrius, he bought it all."

"He bought out Doan?"

"He done did."

"Hell, it's two hundred and fifty miles to the next store," Buchanan said.

"It sure is."

"You got somethin' on your mind, Brownie."

"Waugh." He spat a stream of tobacco juice. "Mebbe."

"Don't keep me in suspenders," Buchanan suggested. "We got to bring this herd over the river and the day's wanin' on us."

The deep eyes twinkled. "You mind the Blackfoot that time years agone?"

"Your father-in-law?"

"Waugh. He like to've skelped me clean."

"All I did was wake you up," Buchanan said.

"And stood off his bunch. Waugh . . . I got supplies."

"You got what?" Buchanan couldn't believe his ears. Brownie had been drifting for years since the end of the buffalo and beaver trade, barely existing as hunter and guide.

"Washed some dust," Brownie said proudly. "Up the Colorado. Come down and heard about you and the woman and her cows. Talk's all up and down the trail. Demetrius and them— they tried to git it outa me where my cache is. Damn near done it, only I tapped a few and they run." He touched the long Bowie. "Skagg, he don't stand too tall."

Buchanan said, "I'll swim the herd over pronto. You fill the wagon with what you got and can spare. I'll pay."

"Shore you'll pay," said Brownie. "What it's wuth, not a penny more. Nor less. I got to get me to Fort Worth and my li'l fling. But I won't hornswoggle you none."

"Just get the vittles ready," Buchanan said. He rode back toward the riverbank. Brownie vanished. Tom Fool was already in the water and the docile herd followed. Porado stayed with the chuck wagon as they swam it over, and brought it up the high-sloped bank of the low-lying river. Then he went back to help with the rest of the herd.

Lu said, "Sure glad to get here, pardner. Vittles is gettin' real low. Where's the store?"

"Never mind the store," Buchanan said. "Demetrius cleaned it out. Us bein' so late it wasn't a big job, at that. Plus a good Samaritan happened to be along."

"I don't know any Samaritans, do I?" she asked dubiously.

"Like in the Bible," he said, waving an arm. "Also, somethin' about bread cast upon the waters."

"You're away ahead of me," she said. "Do you know where to get some supplies?"

A line of dinky burros came upon the horizon, wobbling under their packs, then pressed steadily toward the waiting chuckwagon. Buchanan watched with pleasure as the mountain man drove them with skill accumulated over the long years.

"Brownie knows," Buchanan said. "You won't have enough to pay for them, though."

"Why not?"

"Mainly because you never did. Nor Porado neither. Prices get high along the trail," Buchanan told her. "Let me deal with Brownie. We'll straighten it out later . . . When we get to Dodge."

She looked hard at him. "Hey. I'm happy to have you for a pardner. I mean, we wouldn't be here if it wasn't for you. But you can't put up all the money and take no pay and . . ."

Buchanan interrupted her. "I aim to bring this herd in. I don't aim for you nor Porado to lose anything. And I don't pretend that I'm goin' to lose. If we get a good price, everything'll square away. Nobody'll get rich but it'll be a start for you and for Porado."

"But you're takin' all the chances," she cried.

"Every day, every damn mile of this trail somebody, everybody is takin' chances," he replied. "Even without that bad bunch up ahead. Now you explain to Porado and I'll go and dicker with Brownie. I got a notion he's goin' to make us pay for a broken arm and a black eye."

"A what and a who?"

"Never mind. You get it straight with Porado, count the cash you got left, add up your figures. I'll handle this cash deal."

Suddenly there were tears in her eyes. "Damn it, Tom. You're too good. It ain't right you should take all this on yourself."

"Forget it," he told her. He grinned. "It ain't every springtime I get to travel all these miles with a pretty lady."

He rode off toward the oncoming line of burros before she could reply. He hoped Brownie had corralled enough canned peaches to make a few pies. He knew there would be beans and baking powder and all the necessities, including the terrible coffee bean so beloved by men of the trail. It was the delicacies he craved.

They had been lucky this time. Brownie had appeared in the nick of time. With the dry spell coming on, Buchanan felt it would be all Demetrius and his company could do to take the big herd safely to railhead. From now on it would be a case of survival of the fittest, which meant the survival of the people with the most know-how, and the will to contend with the drudgery of the coming hot, dry days.

SEVEN

BUCHANAN and the Apache boy roamed the country-side. The sun stood steady, defiantly, out of season. The way became dust-dry. Tongues lolled, steers staggered. Pregnant cows dropped calves and then dropped beside them. The ribs of horses and cattle showed through the hides.

Day after day went by. The scouting pair returned to the herd which was ending its slow, painful ten miles at eventide. Texas Kid and Coco, both thinner and weaker than seemed possible, sipped their meager ration of water.

Lulu Lacy, skin roughened and deeply tanned, cooked over a fire from which everyone else kept a safe distance. Porado and his men were riding the restless, wondering, thirsty herd.

Buchanan said, "The land is scorched. It's like some-body burned away every blade of grass, all the water."

"Can we make the Washita?" asked Lu.

"Nearest I can see, it'll be nip and tuck. Mostly tuck," Buchanan answered.

Coco muttered, "Good trainin'," he said. "Get a man

in shape. In shape for a coffin, sez I."

"We melted all the fat off you," Buchanan said.

"I didn't have no fat to begin with," protested Coco. But he went back to his job. They all knew the thirst, they all knew the hard work of the grind. None quit, not for a minute. It was a hard-bitten little group.

They pushed on. They wrung out the last drop of morning dew, they scanned the sky for dark clouds, until their necks ached from the stretching. And they kept going.

There was some liquid in the cans; tomatoes, peaches that no longer were destined to be pies. Lu used the dish water several times, and finally, for her own meager ablutions. The jug of glycerin and rose water dwindled.

Buchanan stayed with the herd now. Every man was needed to keep the gaunt cattle in hand. Even old Tom Fool wavered and wandered and had to be shown the straight way for the Washita and Kansas. Still no human on the drive faltered.

They made one more camp. The wheels on both wagons had dried so that the spokes were shrunken. Buchanan cut leather shims and Texas Kid and Luis Apache turned to with quick young hands to help. Coco rode herd with Dude and Dutch. At the cook fire Porado lingered, trying to lend a helping hand to Lu Lacy, who was still spunky and still could laugh.

They ate, chewing every morsel for the liquid it might contain, never quite satisfied. Afterwards, Buchanan sat with Porado and Lu, apart from the others.

Lu said, "I'm down to the bottom of the water barrel."

"You been down there."

"This time it's the end." She had squirreled water, doling it out in the tin cups, for days upon days.

Porado looked at Buchanan. "What do you think?"

"We push on. Tomorrow might do it."

"Tomorrow?" Lou was amazed. "We're that close?"

"That close," Buchanan said. "I've been expectin' some sort of attack from Demetrius."

"We've been staggering along and didn't realize how far we'd come," Porado said. "Like doing time. You do one day at a time. Just one day, then another."

"Don't talk about that!" Lu said sharply. "Don't go around tellin' people you were in jail."

Porado gave her one of his rare smiles. "I'm not telling everybody, Lu. Just my friends."

Buchanan chuckled. "Come to think of it, that's where I met Coco. We both escaped from jail."

"You did not!" said Lu Lacy. "You're funnin' us."

"Sure did. Down El Paso," Buchanan told them. "There is a Ranger captain don't like me. Good man, but he just don't cotton to me and Coco. It's a long story."

"Tell us."

He told them, relishing the tale of how he had tossed Coco out the jailhouse window, he himself following closely behind. They listened, and when they started to drowse, he finished it off quickly. They bade each other sleepy goodnights and Lu went to the wagon and Porado to his blankets . . . not too far from where she slept.

Buchanan went to the picket line and spoke to Nightshade. He had rested the black, riding three other horses through the long, hot day. Now it was time to saddle up once more and scout the prairie between the camp and the Washita. He was too wide awake to seek his blankets, and the fears lingered—he did not underestimate the enemy. Demetrius had been silent too long.

Nightshade moved swiftly over the plain. In a few hours he covered more than the herd could manage in a long day. There was no sign of anything alive, human or beast, along the entire route.

This alone was enough to alarm Buchanan. Night creatures should have been rustling among the sage, the few clumps of buffalo grass that had survived the drought. Birds should have sprung up beneath the hoofs of the black horse.

He came to the river. It was running strong but at low ebb, of course. He drank and watered Nightshade. He sat in silence for long minutes. The stars vanished and at long last there were clouds scudding, playing their games in the lowering sky.

There would be rain. The herd would reach the river and the water would be welcome, but it was ironic that the storm should be so delayed. Up ahead somewhere Demetrius and his gang must be laughing up their sleeves, Buchanan thought. But how far up ahead? What was the plan nurtured in the head of the vainglorious Greek?

Buchanan tried to figure it out. He had encountered his share of bad men. He had fenced with them, fought with them, beaten them at their own games. Now he tried to imagine what Demetrius had in store for them when the herd hit the Washita on the last leg of the journey to Dodge City over the Western Trail.

Whatever it was, he decided, it would happen after the rains came. There was nothing to do but wait it out.

It was late when the herd smelled the water ahead. Where it had ambled, staggering, it was now trotting. A lowing sound arose on the air. It had been a long drive, but now it was worth every minute. Tom Fool led them straight to the riverbank where they sloshed in, crowding so that the herders had to ride hard to stretch them out lest they drown each other.

They made a big fire. All were dripping wet. Lu Lacy had the coffee on and was trying to prepare a hot meal. It had turned cool in the night and the thunderheads still gathered threateningly above the scene. Buchanan watched the steam rise from his damp clothing and spoke to Porado.

"They'll be logey in the morning."

"We might rest them a day."

"Uh-huh. That's what I thought," replied Buchanan. "If we can hold 'em durin' the storm we won't lose much."

"Will it be a big storm?" Lu asked.

"Texas weather, only a fool can guess what it might be," Buchanan said. "So . . . I guess a big storm."

"But possibly a quick one," Porado ventured. "The wind is high and strong."

"Could be. Best to tie down everything, though," Buchanan said. "Stand double watches. Lightnin' has a way of settin' on the horns of cattle, you mind?"

"I remember," said Porado. "Scares them. Little balls of fire. The Indians had a name for them."

"The Indians have names for every bit of nature," said Buchanan. "Like they invented it all. Which they believe."

Texas Kid and Luis Apache came to the fire, wringing out their garments and laughing together. Lu had the coffee ready for them. Buchanan watched them for a moment, remembering how they had detested one another at journey's beginning. The trail had its compensations, he had often reminded himself.

Porado hitched at his belt and Buchanan joined him, cutting out a fresh mount for each of them. Nightshade made his usual fuss, but he was weary from the hard day, well fed and watered, Buchanan knew.

Porado asked, "Do you think they're waiting for us?"

"Demetrius and his bunch? They're up to somethin', you can bet on that."

"Yes. I feel it in my bones."

"There was no sound, not any, when I got here. I didn't see anybody or anything but the storm wasn't that close. It didn't seem right," Buchanan told him.

"There's nothing to do but keep a watch. We've come this far despite everything. If we make this crossing and Demetrius leaves us alone—we'll get to Dodge in good condition."

"It means a lot to you," said Buchanan.

"It means a new start."

"In this country nobody asks questions," Buchanan agreed. "A small start can become a whole new way of life."

"It means the same to Lu."

"That's why I'm here," Buchanan reminded him. "For the sake of Lu."

"She thinks you're the greatest man alive," Porado said. There was a trace of envy in his voice. "No one could be more grateful."

Buchanan shook his head. "Hey, a man don't want thanks. Not from friends."

"Appreciation? Anyone wants appreciation."

"Uh-huh. Maybe. Look, I feel like I ought to make a scout across the river."

"It's a risk. When the rains hit there'll be a current running hard and high."

"When it begins to rain, have everybody ridin'," Buchanan said. "Can't have another stampede. The buyers in Dodge won't wait forever."

"Not for a small herd like ours," said Porado. "But I sort of hate to see you go over yonder."

"We've got to know. If they've got an ambush planted, maybe we can break it up one more time."

"I still don't like it."

"You watch the cattle. I'll watch Demetrius. It's best this way." He saluted and grinned, and put a big buckskin horse he had chosen for the trip into the water. It was a tough buckskin but no swift runner, he knew. It swam strongly, and they reached the far side of the Washita without incident. It was at that moment when the first raindrop struck on his sombrero.

He unpacked his poncho, stuck his head through the hole in its middle and adjusted the brim of the Stetson against the coming storm. There was a burst of jagged white across the sky and thunder rumbled as loud as the sound of distant artillery. It would be a dandy, he thought. The buckskin shied and he reined in, talking in its cocked ear, soothing it.

The buckskin walked as if afraid to get its feet wet. Buchanan settled down to watch for a sign with the next flash of lightning. He had a notion how far ahead the Demetrius drive would be, but he could not be sure.

He found himself thinking of the crew he had left at the camp. Texas Kid and Luis Apache had come through with flying colors. Dutch and Dude had not changed an iota. That was the way he had found it to be with men—and women too, for that matter. You saw some change their ways, and others tread their single-minded way to dusty death.

Then there was Lu Lacy—and Porado. It occurred to him that he never had heard Porado's first name. Both of them had a past they would like to forget.

Yet neither of them, in Buchanan's book, had anything of which to be ashamed. Each was a victim of time and tide, which plays no favorites for anyone. Porado had never claimed that he was innocent of stealing cattle, but Marshal Doud had left no doubt that there was much to indicate that he was innocent.

Lu was . . . Lulu Lacy, a lady who had seen seamy days, whose heart had been worn on a slightly soiled sleeve. Buchanan well knew that all this was surface, that beneath the veneer dwelt a fine and brave woman, a woman with brains and imagination. He had known many females in his life, up and down the frontier over the past twenty years, and Lu rated up there with the best of them.

The rain continued. It pelted, turned briefly to hail, then settled into a downpour. The buckskin lowered its head and plodded on into the blackness.

Buchanan thought of Coco Bean, for several years now his best and closest friend. They had been together on and off since the episode in El Paso. Now Coco had endured the discomforts and dangers of the trail drive for no other reason than to be with Buchanan. Of course Coco also longed for the day he could get his big partner to face him in a boxing match. Nothing would ever convince him that Buchanan was the better fist fighter.

Buchanan would not dispute him, but neither would he fight him. It was no part of a peaceable man's nature to fight a friend, he told both Coco and himself.

He chuckled. There was a flash so close it temporarily blinded him. There was a searing, white hot thrust of a flaming sword. The buckskin reared, then bolted, disappearing into the storm. Buchanan was flung into the air. He came down like a scorched bundle of old clothes, his head striking a rock. He rolled over and over in deepest blackness.

Lu Lacy yanked at the belt around her narrow waist. The jeans were soaked. It was a most uncomfortable feeling. She saw Porado coming toward her. She could make out his sturdy, medium-sized form against the tiny flame of the smoldering fire.

He said, "They're stirring around."

"The fireballs on their horns. A sight to see."

"One of nature's little tricks. It spooks them a bit. It wouldn't take much to start 'em."

She said, "I'll catch up a horse."

"Take the dun with the blaze," he suggested. "It's a nice, easy going pony."

"If I can tell one from t'other in the dark." She laughed. "Somethin' wild about a storm, ain't there?"

"Wild?" He paused, then said, "Wild, yes. And dangerous. If they start, don't try to turn them. Just ride the rim, stay out of the way of them. Don't shoot, it only excites them more. Too many people been killed trying to turn a stampede with a gun."

"Okay," she said. "You watch yourself, too, you hear?"

"Thank you." He said it from the heart and for a moment the two of them stood in the midst of clanking horns, drumming rain, and all the sounds of a storm, and heard each other clearly, as though in church. It was just an instant, but it was a beginning.

She went to the cavvy, such as it was, and sought the dun. She could not pick it out. She had a light saddle on her shoulder and the ground was turning muddy and slippery. She twisted at the belt into which she had thrust her light revolver. She heard horses coming and turned to see who was in this part of the camp where they would not be of any help in holding the herd.

A man swung down from the saddle. Before she could speak he had grabbed her and struck her alongside the head. She reached for her pistol, screaming against the drumming of the rain, the hammer of lightning.

Bull Skagg said, "Gotcha this time, you prime bitch!"

He hit her again. Morgan, Gotch and Krause were bellowing and swinging blankets, harrassing the herd. Each drew and fired. The steers whined and their horns struck together and they lost all sense of time and place. Tom Fool went down and they ran over him and around him, out of hand and going up river with all the speed they could muster.

Lulu was fighting a losing battle. "I'd scrag yuh right now if I didn't have orders," he was snarling, twisting her arm behind her back. She kicked at him and he hit her with his fist. The blow landed on her chin and she went down into the mud, unconscious.

Skagg picked up her saddle and threw it on the nearest horse. That it happened to be the dun was sheer coincidence. He flopped her across the saddle on her belly and tied her hands and feet to keep her from falling off. Then he rode for the Washita, leading animal and burden.

The herd was off and really stampeding now. Krause and Gotch and Morgan splashed out of the river and caught up with their leader.

He yelled, "You see that damn Buchanan anywhere?"

"Nope."

"Then ride like hell. Tell the boss I got the whore."

They rode. Skagg followed at a slower gait. It was not that he cared whether Lu Lacy suffered. It was because he was scared of Demetrius.

Buchanan thought he was dead, banished to a deep dark limbo. He was blind, his head ached enormously, he could not move and there was a terrible banging somewhere nearby. He was also wet to the knees, but dry above the waist.

It took him some time to realize that he was wrapped in the folds of the poncho and that his hat was jammed over his face. He kicked once or twice and was able to roll over and get to his knees.

He sat for a moment, gathering strength. The rain still poured down. He staggered once, twice, nearly fell. He took a deep breath. The buckskin, spooked by the lightning, was gone.

The river was back that way, he thought, behind him. Buchanan stumbled forward. After a few strides, he got his rhythm back and was walking in a straight line. There was no way to fret about Demetrius now, the important matter was a new mount—Nightshade, if he was lucky.

He had gone a half mile when there was a whinnying sound directly ahead of him in the blackness, amidst the downpour. He dropped to one knee and waited, tension rising. He held his breath, doubting that a friendly horseman would be riding this side of the Washita.

The dim bulk came on. Now there was a high, keen note to the call of the horse. Buchanan yelped.

"Nightshade!"

The black came close, whinnying a complaint. He nuzzled Buchanan where he knelt in the mud.

Buchanan said, "What in the world you doin' this side of the river? Wait—don't tell me. There's trouble, and plenty of it."

He ran his hand over the horse, making sure there was no injury, no break in the hide. Satisfied, Buchanan swung bareback onto his faithful horse. It was not necessary to point Nightshade to the river; he always knew the way to go. In a short time they were fighting the current, already running strong, getting back to the herd.

The camp was unquestionably a shambles. A few of the cavvy wandered about, aimlessly, wonderingly. Buchanan managed to line up most of them, linking them with two ropes which were twisted, soaking near the fire. Listening, he heard the sounds of riders and cattle. It came from the west. There had been a stampede, then. Everyone was out trying to break it, to bring back the herd. He climbed aboard Nightshade and rode out to greet them and to ascertain the damage.

Porado was riding the point. Tom Fool, white spots visible in the gloom, plodded ahead, and the weary cattle followed him. The riders rode them in a circle to the bedding grounds from whence they had started. It was muddy now but they would hold, wearied from their run. Buchanan rode back to the tiny remnants of fire and tried to stir it up. He brought out his faithful dark lantern and applied a taper from his oilskin pack. A feeble glow illuminated the near scene as Porado, gaunt and wasted, came into view.

Buchanan rummaged in the chuck wagon and found some dry mesquite kindling. He threw it on the fire. The rain continued. He arranged a tarp from the supply wagon and the little flames grew.

"Everybody accounted for?" was his first question.

"Haven't had time to count. They gave us a hell of a

99

run. Couldn't turn 'em to the river, so it was all one way," said Porado wearily.

Texas Kid came into the firelight. He had a bruise over one eye. He took off his hat and showed it in the light of Buchanan's lantern. There was a bullet hole in it.

He said, "Somebody started 'em. They was tired and full of water. They would've stood. Someone stampeded them."

"Someone near killed you, that's for sure," said Buchanan.

"I heard a yell. It wasn't none of us," insisted the Kid.

"Better start countin' noses," said Buchanan. He spoke lightly to conceal the sudden worry he felt. He had not seen Coco. Now he looked around and asked, "Did Lu ride out with y'all?"

"She was going to pick up that dun, you know the one. She wanted to ride. I never did see her, though," said Porado.

"Me neither," said Texas Kid.

"I'll have a look. You men get some rest if you can," Buchanan said.

He mounted Nightshade and they started a wide circle. He found Dutch and Dude still riding but getting ready to come in. He found Coco at the far side of the herd, hunched in the saddle, not quite sure of what course to take.

"You go on in and get coffee," said Buchanan.

"Coffee? Don't even say it. Man, you really tryin' to get me kilt, ain't you?"

"Now, friend, you're alive and well, ain't you?"

"Be careful how you call me your friend," said Coco. "That arrangement might just end before this is over."

"Did you see Lu ridin' the little dun anywhere along the way?"

"No and I hope she wasn't there," said Coco. "It was, believe me, no place for a lady."

Buchanan rode on. The muddy trail was easy to follow. He began to cast it, from side to side. He dreaded what he might find—a little pony down, a woman injured or dead.

He rode the entire distance covered by the stampede. He found nothing. Not even a head of cattle had gone down, it appeared. He turned back toward camp, making a wider swing across the trail. In the end, he knew she had not gone down beneath the hoofs of the herd.

She could, of course, have gone into the river. His heart was heavy as lead when he returned to the fire where the others awaited him.

Kid Texas had a pot of beans and some beef heating beneath the tarpaulin. The rain slacked for a few moments as they all stared at Buchanan, half in fear, half in grief.

Porado said in a monotone, "I won't believe it."

"She was a hell of a nice lady," the Kid said, his eyes large and round.

Luis Apache picked up Buchanan's little dark lantern and began circling around the chuck wagon and the fire. Buchanan dipped out beans. They did not taste right; he picked at them. He said to Porado, "I don't want to believe it, neither."

"Maybe she's just done lost herself," Coco offered.

"No. She's not lost. The dun would bring her in if she got turned around," said Buchanan.

Porado asked suddenly, "Where's the buckskin?"

Buchanan told them what had happened. "The horse musta been scared off. Probably will never make it back to camp, poor animal."

Coco said, "You ain't ready for the good Lord, Tom Buchanan. He don't want you, that's purely right."

Kid Texas said, "You was over the river. You didn't see nobody?"

"No. But . . . there was a feelin'. You know?" He thought back. "Uh-huh. A feelin' that there was somethin' out there."

"I heard that guy yell," insisted Kid Texas. "I know it wasn't none of us."

"There's no way to track in this rain," Buchanan said. "We could ride but we wouldn't know where to. I didn't even locate the camp of Demetrius before I got hit."

There was a loud cry from the edge of the campfire

light where Luis Apache prowled. "¡*Hola*! See what I have found!"

Buchanan put down the tin plate and was at his side in two bounds. Luis held up a wet and muddy weapon. It was Lu's revolver.

Buchanan said, "She might've dropped it when she climbed onto the dun."

"No. Look here." Luis shone the lamp upon the ground. The cavvy had bolted in a westerly direction. This place was relatively unmarked by hoofs. There were deep-set tracks. Luis knelt, telling the story in mixed Spanish and Apache, talking to Buchanan. "You see this horse? This is not of our horses. This is a horse of a stranger. Here are other tracks. I know the tracks of our horses. These are not of them. Here, see where they rode? To fire those shots, to stampede the herd."

Buchanan said, "And here they turn and go to the river. These are the tracks of the stranger."

"And of the dun!" cried Luis Apache. "The strange horse and the dun. They go to the river, no?"

Buchanan arose. He said heavily, "They go to the river, yes. But they're flushed away now. There's been too much rain."

"I will ride with you," said Luis Apache. "I will find where the dun horse and the strange horse go."

"Yes," said Buchanan. "Me and Porado. You'll ride with us. Let's put it this way—we'll ride with you."

They saddled up. Porado had very little to say. He was struggling, Buchanan guessed, with a deep and hurting fear. Texas Kid for once made no objection. He and Coco and the other pair would watch the weary herd.

Buchanan had no doubt that Lulu had been kidnapped. Apaches made no mistakes about signs that others could never translate. Luis had proven himself again and again. The problem was how to rescue her.

There were nearly a score of men in the camp of Demetrius. The ones who had been left behind to die on the hilltop were not real gunners. Skagg and his bullies, Spandau and his tough riders, were not likely to leave the camp unguarded.

It was necessary to scheme. Porado was too involved, too emotional to come up with ideas. Luis Apache might do better, but he was a lad in his teens. It was up to Buchanan, and he knew it very well indeed. He led them into the river.

They had rigged a tarp, pegging it so that it sheltered the carriage from the rain. There was an Indian-style fire, which gave heat without emitting too much smoke. Demetrius sat on the upholstered seat with a glass of wine in one hand and a fat chicken leg in the other. He snickered at Lulu Lacy.

"You see? You always make the wrong move. Now look at you!"

Never had a more bedraggled captive woman stood before her enemy. She had lost her hat long since. Her hair was a tangled mass of damp strands. Her middle ached from the tortures of the ride across the saddle so that she could not straighten up. Her face was swollen from the blows administered by Skagg. They had tied her hands because she had, upon arriving at the camp, scratched Skagg from eye to chin so that he still bled as he cursed her under his breath and promised dire happenings for her, before her death by hanging.

Demetrius said, "You think Skagg was exaggerating, do you? What about my men who were slaughtered? You are guilty as much as those who fired the bullets, believe me."

She said, "You are a gutless fat belly, ain't you, Demetrius? Really a bastard."

He smiled. "Whatever you say doesn't matter. You don't matter. You think I crave your favors? A pig like you? Worn down to the bone working for saddle bums?"

"When those bums catch up with you I just want to be alive enough to see it," she told him.

"Oh, we've thought of that." He beamed, bit at the chicken, sipped the wine. "If they come near us, you will be shot before their very eyes."

"And if they don't—you'll hang me? Now, that's a

fine choice." She laughed at him. "Further and more, if you dared to hang a woman, you wouldn't live out the year. Don't you know that much about the country?"

"I know that when we get through telling our story about you—even a Buchanan would agree that you deserved hanging." He laughed. "Buchanan! A fool. A huge body without brains."

"If you had half his brains you might be a hundredth of what you think you are," she said contemptuously.

"We shall see about that, won't we?" He finished the wine and called, "Skagg!"

The scratch was red along Skagg's nose. He glared at Lulu, saying, "Yes, Boss? Can I scrag her now?"

"Of course not. Would I go out into the rain to see it done?" Demetrius laughed again. "Just see that she don't get away. No food, no water. Just watch her. Tie her up like a dog. She don't matter to me any more. But I want her alive, you understand?"

Skagg leered. "The boys sure crave a little fun. The rain wouldn't bother them none. We could wash her up a bit."

Demetrius considered. Then he said, "That's not a bad idea. It might take some of the pride out of her. But don't rush it. Let her think about it for awhile. And keep her hands tied. If she gets away—I'll have your hide, you know."

Skagg grabbed Lulu by the hair. "Come on, you bitch. No wonder the boss don't wantcha. Monk and Bowie and Butch, they ain't partic'lar, that's for sure."

Demetrius watched as he dragged her outdoors into the rain. Beau Spandau came from behind the carriage where he had been hiding.

"I'm all for the ladies," he said, drawling a bit. "This here, though, it ain't a man's game."

"You work for me. You don't ask questions," said Demetrius. "You get the cattle through. You watch for Buchanan. Is that understood?"

"Just wanted you to know. The woman's got guts," said Spandau. "I don't mind killin' when it's necessary. But this other business, I don't want any part of it."

"Nobody asked you to take part in it."

Spandau said, "Let 'em take her where I can't see nor hear it," Spandau said. "Otherwise me or my men, we might have to take a hand."

"You can tell Skagg," said Demetrius. He needed Spandau to get his herd through. Once in Dodge, with the situation well in hand, he could deal with such as Spandau, he thought. There were always more guns for hire. He shrugged as the boss herder left, and poured himself more whiskey. He finished the chicken. When Skagg and the others went to work on Lulu he would wrap himself in a raincoat slicker and sneak out and watch. He would thus have a most enjoyable day, thanks to the rain and the working of his marvelously clever brain.

Buchanan stayed in the saddle, making sure his revolver and ammunition were dry beneath the poncho. The rain continued, a steady pace now, without bolts of lightning to guide them. Luis Apache seemed oblivious to the elements, sheltering the little lantern, forever quartering and backtracking, trying to find the remnants of the trail of the herd ahead.

Porado began to talk, softly, to Buchanan. "We don't even know they've got her."

"Take it from me. They've got her."

"If they have . . ." He broke off, inhaling.

Buchanan said, "Uh-huh. I know what you mean."

"She's such a—a dead game woman."

"Good lookin', too," said Buchanan. "All wool and a yard wide and handsome to boot. I know, Porado. I know."

"But they could be . . ."

Buchanan interrupted, "And probably are. You got to get it out of your mind, man. You got to think on pullin' her out of it."

"I know, but . . ."

"She's no delicate prairie flower," said Buchanan with deliberate sharpness. "She'll survive."

"That's a hell of a thing for you to say. She worships the ground you walk on," retorted Porado.

"And you're no farmer boy," Buchanan went on. "So get yourself together, Porado, or you'll be no use to us."

Luis Apache came running, jumped aboard his pony. "There is the trail. Straight north. No east, no west. Straight north. Not too far."

"Uh-huh," said Buchanan. He looked at Porado in the dark and said aloud, "I should have brought Coco. He's better at close work. There's enough guns up yonder to blow us to hell the minute we're discovered. Get that into your heads, you two."

Porado did not answer.

Luis Apache said brightly, "I think this is Indian job, no?"

"Somewhat," said Buchanan. "Only not so much hoo-raw, if you know what I mean."

"Truly Apache way?" asked the boy in Spanish.

"Truly."

"Then we must ride fast but go quiet?"

"*Sí*, Luis. That is so."

Porado still did not speak. He urged his horse ahead through the rain as though impatient with his companions.

Buchanan said, "A man learns a lot in jail. He becomes a real cool customer. Then he sees a woman that he likes and it all goes plumb to the devil. Or some place where he can't find it."

"What is it you say?" asked Luis Apache.

"Never mind. Just keep Porado in sight. We will think about things after we survey the camp, you savvy?"

"I savvy good," said Luis. "I have got the little pistol. It is clean and dry. It will not make much noise."

"Have you got that knife?"

"Oh, but yes, *Señor* Tom."

"It makes less noise. Now let's ride," said Buchanan.

The rain never stopped. The odor of wet horse and saddle blanket rose to their nostrils. In a little while they caught up with Porado. His head was sunk into his collar and the brim of his hat shed water all around. Nobody spoke—it was not a time for talk.

Buchanan thought of the men under Demetrius. They would be scattered—some of them might be making sport with Lulu, but there would be guards riding the herd. He dared not repeat his trick of segregating one of the riders; they might be ready for that.

Yet a diversion was precisely what must be created. It had to be sudden and it had to center around the cattle. Any frontal attack upon the men would surely end in disaster for Lulu and for themselves.

The trail became plainer. Luis swung down to test the temperature of the dung left by the cattle. He said, "Very soon now. Best we got quiet, now."

They went as quietly as possible. Dimly they saw the bulk of cattle, some down in the mud, most standing with lowered heads facing away from the wind. The rain poured down. Buchanan reined in and the others came close, barely able to distinguish one another.

Buchanan said, "Scout it. Luis, you take the herd. If there's any way to move 'em without givin' yourself away—go to it. Porado, you circle the camp, get everything you can into your head."

They obeyed from habit. Buchanan had spotted something he did not want Porado to see, a drift of wood smoke coming from the east. He rode Nightshade as close as he dared and knew he had found the chuck wagon and the carriage which sheltered Demetrius. A fire was built where there should not have been a fire. It was protected from the rain, but flickering and throwing little light. He dismounted and moved through the mist and the rain, silent as a grizzly.

There were lanterns, he now saw, held under coats by a group of men. There was the sound of raucous laughter. Buchanan crept closer. No one was on guard here, everyone was hugely entertained by the fun.

They had Lu Lacy tied to the wheel of a wagon. Skagg was ripping the shirt from her back. Monk Morgan threw a bucket of icy water over her torso.

"Clean up the hoor, then lemme have her!" someone yelled.

She faced them. She held her head high even as her teeth chattered so that she could not curse them aloud.

One came too close and she kicked at his crotch and he ducked away, laughing.

Skagg took advantage, trying to get at her belt to rip off the Levi's. Again she kicked. Buchanan's gun was in his hand, he was shaking as hard as was Lulu. He was grateful that he had sent Porado off on the long tour —but he knew the ex-con would be coming full circle any moment. There would be hell to pay—and they would lose and Lulu would die if Porado came shooting.

Buchanan moved again. He saw the canvas shelter of the carriage billowing. He was close enough to reach out and touch it. He waited, holding his breath, making a small, soundless prayer.

A bulky figure emerged from the canvas. There was a low, loud chuckle. Demetrius was smoking a cigar, protecting it from the rain with a fat palm.

Skagg yelled, "Just gimme a little time. I'll get her ready. And I'm first, y'all mind that!"

Demetrius laughed. As he did Buchanan's huge hand closed over his mouth, crushing the cigar so that it burnt into the cheek of the helpless victim.

Buchanan said, "Whisper a damn word and you're dead."

Demetrius moaned. Buchanan whisked the cigar away. He pressed the Colt's cold muzzle into the left ear of Demetrius.

"Fun's over. Call 'em off. Have her brought here. Make one bad move and you'll roast in hell so quick you won't know what hit you."

Demetrius nodded vigorously. Buchanan took his hand away from the slobbering mouth.

"Hurry, man. If they pull one more dirty trick I'll make it six of you dead."

Demetrius started forward, calling hoarsely, "Skagg!"

Buchanan yanked him back. "Stay right here where we can see them and they can't see us."

"Skagg!"

The man turned, his head lowered like the bull for which he was called. "What you want, boss?"

"The woman."

A shout of anger went up. Voices chorused, "Hey, you promised us! We got 'er ready, boss. It ain't fair!"

"So you promised 'em?" Buchanan said. "Get her over here with her clothes on and be damn quick about it."

Demetrius said, "I changed my mind. Understand? I want her here. Give her the shirt and her coat."

"I suppose you want me to cut her loose, too." Skagg was on the edge of defiance.

It could all fall apart in an instant, Buchanan knew. If the men revolted—or if Porado appeared—the fat would surely be in the fire. He shoved the muzzle of the gun sharply in Demetrius's ear. "Just send her here."

Demetrius said, "Put her shirt on and send her here. You go about your business."

"Hey, that don't make no sense," Skagg howled. "She's a hellcat with her hands loose."

"You do as I say." Blood was trickling now from where the gun sight had cut Demetrius inside his ear.

Skagg said, "It's a rotten trick. I don't care what you say, it ain't square."

"That's right. Bull's right," came from the crowd.

"You know who's boss!" Demetrius had gained some vocal power through fear. Skagg reluctantly picked up Lu's shirt, threw it over her shoulders. The buttons on her longjohns were gone and she shrugged in an effort to cover her high, full breasts. She still held herself well, shoulders high, walking toward the sound of the voice of Demetrius.

Skagg yelled, "This here is loco. We don't like this, boss, you might's well know."

A horse came out of the pelting rain. Porado leaned low, his gun in his hand. Skagg had opened his mouth to make another remark. A bullet caught him and drove him over and down.

Guns flashed in the light of the lamps. Buchanan groaned. Lulu began to run. She fell and Buchanan thought she had been shot. He drew back the Colt's and swung it hard against the head of Demetrius. Then he ran forward.

Lu put up her arms. Buchanan lifted her and swept

her back behind the carriage. Porado had made his run and was turning to go again, shooting too fast for good aim.

Buchanan roared, "Porado!"

The man seemed not to hear. There was a yell from over at the other side of the camp. Then there was a wolf howl, keening to the skies. It was followed by another, this time in a different key. In a moment it seemed a pack of wolves were into the herd, cutting them down.

Porado's gun was empty. He came winging back toward Buchanan, drawing fire. Bullets flew around them all as Buchanan picked up Lu and put her in Porado's arms.

"You done your damned fool best to ruin the play," he said. "Now see if you can get her out of here."

He had no intention of leaving at this juncture. He had recognized the call of the wild. He knew it did not come from the slavering muzzles of wolves—knew in fact that there were no wolves in this country, knew they were for the most part slandered, harmless. When the herd began to stampede in earnest, he climbed aboard Nightshade and began to search for one small Indian youth.

Luis was at the tail end of the running, scared herd. His pony was nearby, trained to follow his master, eager for the new game, whatever it was. Two of the riders came bearing down and Buchanan shot one of them. The other, unable to figure out what was happening, ducked low in the saddle and rode like the wind, away from the herd, leaving the command under Spandau one man less.

Luis was giggling. "It worked! You see it? You hear me?"

Buchanan said, "You took a chance. Your wolf call ain't really all that terrific, you know that?"

"I know it. You know it. But do the dumb cows know it?"

Buchanan said, "I think we ride now. I think it is time to go."

"Our lady, she is safe?"

"I don't know how safe she is. But Porado's got her and he's headed for home. And we better raise the boys

110

and be ready because there might be a small war."

"Big war, small war," said Luis Apache. "I am on your side. We show them war!"

"You're a fine boy," said Buchanan. "You did good with your wolf call. It's good to have you on my side."

But he knew it was hopeless if Demetrius ordered open warfare upon the little crew he was ramrodding. Six guns, including Lulu Lacy, and one fist fighter could not stand off even the depleted army under a smart, tough man like Beau Spandau.

Still, there was a chance. The Demetrius herd was stampeding. And now the rain had stopped. There would be plenty of water coming down from the hills from now on. Grass might be found between the Washita and Dodge City where time had passed since the big herds went through.

They came into the camp. The fire was burning bright now and Texas Kid was cooking and Lu Lacy sat on a cracker box, her shoulders bent. She had donned a clean shirt and Buchanan imagined she had found clean underwear in her gear also. She stared at him.

He said, "No harm done, Lu."

"They shamed me." Her voice was dull. "If you hadn't come along . . ."

"Forget it," he told her.

"Porado saw me."

"I'll say it once more," Buchanan recited with care. "Neither one of you is fresh out of the little red schoolhouse. Now cut it out and get ready to move."

"Move? Are you completely loco?"

"We move at daybreak. It's a couple hours from now. We go over the river and if we can pass Demetrius we'll keep goin'. If he sends guns against us I want to be up in front of him, not waitin' back here. We got the smallest herd. We can outrun him. We can get to Dodge ahead of him. If he don't send the gunners."

"He'll send them. You made him yell calf rope," she said. "They'll come after us."

"Some of 'em won't," Buchanan said grimly. "And some got to stay with the herd after it's gathered up."

She sighed. After a moment she stood up and grinned in the firelight. "You got a way with you, Tom Buchanan. You may be crazy, but you can convince me any time."

"And there's nothin' to be shamed about. You stood up to 'em fine," he said severely.

"I raked that Skagg. Is he dead, you think?"

"I don't know. It happened too quick." He didn't think Porado had killed the man but he thought he knew how Lu felt about it. "If he didn't—somebody will, one time or another."

"He needs it. He needs it bad," she said solemnly. "And Tom—you better talk to Porado."

"Uh-huh. I mean to."

"No, what it is, I told him you had it all set up when he come ridin'."

"He came ridin' because it was you," said Buchanan. "You know that, don't you?"

Now she flushed and turned away from him. "Go on. Talk to him."

"Uh-huh," said Buchanan. He unsaddled Nightshade and led him to the tie line. He walked around the supply wagon. Dutch and Dude were coming in to eat and get some sleep along with Coco. Texas Kid and Luis, youth on their side, were going to ride herd with Porado.

Buchanan called, "Got a minute?"

Porado waited, his head bowed. He said as Buchanan came to him, "I'm sorry."

"You didn't know I had Demetrius."

"It was seeing her there. Like she was. Not giving in to them."

"Yes. She was very good," said Buchanan. "Don't feel bad about it. We got her loose."

"But I might have had her killed. I lost my head. I don't often lose my wits, Buchanan."

"Uh-huh. And you won't next time. I think we better pull out at dawn," said Buchanan. "If they do get their herd together they'll have to take a day to rest."

Porado thought for a moment. Then he replied, "You're right. Best to push ahead and take our chances."

"You know the odds."

"If they come after us? Yes. I saw them. There's more'n a dozen of them left."

"And all gunners."

"All gunners."

Buchanan said, "So we make a run for it now that the cattle is watered."

"Yes. I agree. And . . . I am sorry for what happened."

"Keep it to yourself—and forget it quick as possible," Buchanan advised him. "Lu won't hold it against you."

Porado nodded. "Lu's too big to hold a grudge." He mounted his pony and rode out. Buchanan watched him and thought that he was a good man but that he might well not be able to handle this situation. Lu was an unpredictable woman and she fancied men with dimples.

He was suddenly aware of hunger. He went back to the chuck wagon. Again Lu was wrapped in a blanket, perched on a box, leaning against the rear wheel. She started up, groggy, but Buchanan took her elbow and steered her to the supply wagon. He turned back the tarpaulin. It was dry underneath. He picked her up and put her on the bed of the wagon and pulled the tarp back in place.

She said, "Somebody might be hungry."

"Let 'em eat," said Buchanan. "I told you, get your sleep. We'll be movin' before you know it."

She murmured, "Buchanan?"

"Yes?"

"I couldn't have taken it. Maybe I ain't a newborn chick from the farm. But I couldn't have stood it."

"You didn't have to," he told her gently. "It's all right now."

"But you got it in your mind. You think I'm tough."

"No," he said. "Not tough. Just brave and good."

"I'll go for the first part." She smiled, her eyes closed. "The second part—it's where I'm headin' for. If they let me."

"They'll let you," he said emphatically. "Nobody's goin' to stop you."

He patted her hand and she continued to smile. He went to the fire and ate cold beans and some meat. The

113

biscuits made by Texas Kid were like hunks of iron, so he opened a package of crackers and washed it all down with the black coffee Lu had provided.

He would have to stay awake just in case Demetrius sent gunners. Or at least half awake. He had long since learned to sleep with one eye open and both ears attuned. There were the boys and Porado—and Coco and Dutch and Dude. They all knew the chances. They would all be watching and listening. It was a good, small crew now that it had been broken to the trail. It would be a shame to have it wiped out.

Demetrius coughed. The space underneath the canvas reeked of coal oil from the lanterns and smoke from the Indian fire, which was smouldering.

"Can't you do anything about that fire?" he demanded.

Bowie Gotch, who seemed to have knowledge of rude frontier medicine, shook his head. "Skagg's the onliest one knows how to handle the fire. He stayed with Injuns oncet."

"I don't give a damn who he stayed with!" Demetrius took a deep breath. Already Gotch was scowling because the Greek had complained about the mutton tallow, which now was pasted on the ear that Buchanan had scarred with the muzzle of his gun.

Skagg was stretched on a blanket. Bowie had a small knife and was prodding into his left shoulder. "Little to the right and he'd be a dead ol' Skagg," he said. "I think I got the damn bullet now."

Skagg moaned. He stunk to high heaven of whiskey, which they had poured into him as an anesthetic. He twisted and Gotch swore mildly at him.

"Shoulda kept a couple boys in here to hold him down."

"You know we couldn't do that," said Demetrius. "Not with Buchanan and his gang loose somewhere outside."

"If they are, it wouldn't be no big surprise if they let go a load o' lead into here." Gotch grinned as Demetrius flinched. "But they ain't. They got a herd to attend. Just like Spandau."

"Spandau was right to take his men and go after the

114

herd," Demetrius said. "That's his job."

"Left us hangin', though. Billy's dead out there, where Monk and Butch is buryin him. Skagg here, he ain't gonna be much good for awhile."

Demetrius said feverishly, "All the more reason to push on to Dodge."

"Hah!" grunted Gotch. He held up a bloody hunk of lead. "That's it. Now we'll slap some tallow on him and bandage it up. Better burn it first, though."

He washed the wound with a cloth almost clean, which he dipped in rain water. He stuck the tip of his huge Bowie knife into the fire. He whistled, waiting, watching Skagg, who twitched and muttered and complained in a monotone.

"You'll kill him," Demetrius said. "I don't want him to die in here."

"I don't want him to die nowhere," Gotch said harshly. "I swan, boss, you ain't thinkin' kindly of nobody, are you?"

Demetrius said, "It's that goddam Buchanan. He's every place he's not supposed to be."

"Can't let him get you goin'," Gotch said. "Looks to me like you're spooked."

"I am not afraid. Neither am I a fool," said Demetrius, rising, staring down at the crouching Gotch and the supine Skagg. "I am a businessman. We will get the herd together. We will hold it here. We will go to Dodge City. Then I will deal with Buchanan."

"Yep," said Gotch. "That's a good notion, all right. Skagg will be all right again by then. Skagg'll want another chance at Buchanan."

He pulled the Bowie from the fire. He looked hard at it, saw that it was red hot. He bent over and applied it suddenly to the hole in Skagg's shoulder.

Skagg sat up, screaming in pain. "You dirty, rotten, lousy, misbegotten . . ."

Gotch shoved him back down. He thumbed a gob of mutton tallow from a jar and slapped it on the still sizzling wound. "You gonna be okay if you do like I say. Now just you lay there and drink some more o' this whiskey and tomorrow you'll be up and around. You listen to ol' Gotch."

Skagg fell back down. His eyes closed as Bowie forced whiskey between his lips, but he seemed able to swallow. There was a trace of a drunken grin on his face as he muttered, "Gotch . . . He knows . . . Ol' Gotch . . ."

Demetrius said impatiently, "All right. If you're through with him, get him out of here."

Gotch stood up. "Out of here? Where to?"

Demetrius said, "What do I . . . ?" He broke off. He bit his lip. "One of the wagons," he suggested mildly. "Cover him good and let him sleep it off."

Gotch picked up a blanket. He warmed it over the smoking fire. He placed it carefully around the lower half of Skagg. He fished out a white cloth and began to fashion a pad. He placed the pad upon the wound and wound it with strips of an old sheet which he had in his saddlebag, ready for such contingencies. "He stays right here, boss. You want to sleep in a wagon, you go ahead. Ol' Skagg, he needs to be right quiet and warm."

Demetrius began to object. Then he shut his mouth tightly. He climbed up onto the spring-seat of the carriage and pulled the buffalo robe about him. He said nothing further to Bowie Gotch.

He lay on his injured ear out of long habit, groaned and turned over. Now it would be difficult getting to sleep, he knew. He fumbled around and found the bottle of brandy he kept secreted in the carriage. He swallowed and counted his problems.

It had all gone wrong. Only Spandau had done his job right, going after the cattle with ten or eleven men . . . Demetrius had forgotten the head count, or how many had been killed. He only knew that he owed Buchanan a tremendous score.

At Dodge City he could repair it all. Skagg, Gotch, Morgan and Krause were still alive. They would be his bodyguards. If Spandau wanted in on it, that could be arranged also. Maybe Spandau would be enraged on account of the stampede, knowing Buchanan was behind it. With all these men they could either cut off the herd and kill Buchanan—or handle it all in Dodge. There were more ways than one to get control of the cattle owned by Porado and the woman. Tomorrow his head would stop aching and Demetrius would again be the ruler of all he surveyed. With more to come, he added, a lot more to come. He had only to eliminate that goddam Buchanan . . .

EIGHT

IT WAS NIGHT when they came abreast of the Demetrius herd. They were twenty miles to the east now, and they were worn down. Old Tom Fool, the lead steer, wanted to stop, but Porado brought him smartly along.

Buchanan was riding out on the point, halfway between the two herds of cattle. If Demetrius made an attack he wanted to know it at once. He thought not; he thought the stampede and the shooting and the battering of Demetrius himself would delay that drive.

He well knew what was ahead. He had been up the Western Trail before with a fast traveling herd. The animals would be skin and bones when they hit Kansas. If there were no adequate feeding ground near Dodge City, the herd would have to be driven to Wyoming to fatten up. Otherwise the owners would not get a decent price—and the herders would not be able to collect their wages. Nor would Buchanan be reimbursed.

Worse, a lot of faith would be lost. Time and trouble and the endurance of dangers would have gone for nothing. People often could not stand up under such losses.

He rode further toward the Demetrius course. He neither saw nor heard riders coming his way. Coyotes wailed in the night, seeking little beasts to prey upon since there were no straggling, weak cows or calves. He headed Nightshade for a creek five miles further on.

When he arrived the camp was already made. Coco was eating with Porado and Lu, the others were either catching up on sleep or trying to keep awake while riding night watch.

Coco said, "They comin' after us, Tom?"

"Nope. They're nursin' their wounds." He helped himself to beans and meat. "We've got a half day on 'em right now. Up early tomorrow and we'll be so far ahead they'll never catch up before Dodge."

Coco said, "But if they do catch us, there's me, back on the drag, all by my own self."

"I'll be with you," Buchanan promised.

"It won't help. Guns!" said Coco. "They got plenty of guns."

"Demetrius don't dare send 'em all against us," Buchanan said. "If he should lose, he'd lose everything. Skagg won't be useful for awhile. Spandau is a cattleman and will stay with his job until Kansas."

Porado nodded. "I believe you. Trouble is, we're losin' pounds of beef every hour, now. And a couple of the cows dropped calves today and wouldn't leave them. They'll be food for Demetrius when he catches up to them."

"It's the chance we got to take," Buchanan insisted. "There's no other way. Stay behind them and they got us blocked every which way."

"He's right," said Lu. "I can see it. If we're ahead we get the choice of graze and water. And we can protect us better, makin' them do the catchin' up."

"Yes. It's the only way." Porado sighed. "I'm going to hate to bring out a buyer when we get to Dodge, though. We'll have a lot of skinny beef."

"I'm not guaranteein' Demetrius won't make a raid on

us," Buchanan admonished them. "I'm just trying to play percentages."

"It's the gambler's choice," Lu said.

"All I want's to get to where we're goin' and sleep," Coco said. "You 'member talkin' about a fight up there, Tom?"

"I remember."

"Forget it. I ain't gonna fight nobody no time until I get all this here trip so far behind me I can't recall one hour of it." He stretched, yawned, reached for his blankets, which had been drying beside the fire, and went off to find a dry place to sleep.

"First time I ever heard him talk like that," said Buchanan. "Mostly he'd rather fight than eat."

"In the prize ring, you mean," said Lulu. "Outside, he's the most peaceable man I know."

"You're wrong there," Buchanan said. "I'm the most peaceable man you know. It's just that people like y'all lead me into trouble."

"I can't deny that," Porado said. "This drive has been nothing but."

"We're gettin' there," Buchanan told him. "If we hold on tight enough we'll make it."

"You and all the rest of 'em have been wonderful," said Lu. "I reckon a woman is sure enough bad luck on a trail drive like they say. But you men have done the best anybody could."

She smiled faintly at them and went to the wagon where she slept. Porado and Buchanan watched her as she climbed wearily into her canvas nest.

Buchanan said, "She's all there."

Porado still watched. "She's the best I ever knew."

"Keep that thought in mind," Buchanan advised him. "Meantime, get some sleep. Eat, sleep and ride, that's the program for now."

"Good night," said Porado. "And thanks—for everything."

"Uh-huh." Buchanan found his sougan and went to where Coco was nestled beneath the chuck wagon.

"What did go on, anyhow?" Coco asked.

Buchanan told him, remembering every detail as it had unreeled before his eyes. Coco listened until it was ended. Then he spoke in solemn turns.

"That Demetrius, he gonna be after you. Man like that, he seems like he's yella. Maybe he is. I mind a few fighters in the ring like that. Duck and run and grab. Then they slug you when you're down, or on one knee or in the ropes. Mean. Men like that are mean."

"Uh-huh. And mean bosses attract mean men," Buchanan said. "That Beau Spandau, he's a good cattleman. But he's a dude and he'll shoot you for the luck of it."

"I don't know him. But I know people like Demetrius. There's a heap of 'em around. Some in high places," said Coco.

"They can fool a lot of the people some of the time," Buchanan agreed. "But remember what Mr. Lincoln said.'

"Mr. Lincoln, he said the slaves was free," Coco observed. "That may be. But none of us walkin' the sidewalk when a white man wants the road."

"That'll change," Buchanan prophesied. "Sooner or later, it's all got to change."

"But you and me, we won't live to see the day," Coco said without rancour. "Things is as they be and the best way is to go 'long as far as you can with 'em."

"Anyway," Buchanan observed sleepily, "you never was a slave."

"Nope, I never was. And I'm a champeen," said Coco softly. "And I thank the good Lord for his blessin'."

He was asleep immediately, curled under his blanket. Buchanan watched him for a moment, marveling at the simplicity and decency and courage of his friend. Give the country a few thousand more like Coco Bean, he thought, and all would be well in the best of all possible worlds.

He fell asleep believing this, and awakened as he had planned before daybreak, before the others were aroused, helping Lu with the fire, whispering to her.

"I'll take some bread and meat. Got to go backtrack a ways and make sure they ain't sendin' a posse."

"You'll get yourself killed yet, Tom Buchanan," she

121

scolded. But she made him a huge packet of food and he filled his canteen and saw to his ammunition. He carried the six-gun in the holster, a spare in his belt, strange procedure for a peaceable man. But he knew the chance of being cornered and he was determined to sell out dearly.

Nightshade was rested. The black horse never seemed weary. Buchanan saddled up and rode southward.

The sun came boldly after the rains, showing a golden finger, then lining the clouds with pink and white so that they floated high. Buchanan came to a rise in the ground and sat there taking it all in, the wide plain, the scene painted for him above his head.

He said, "There'll be towns and farms and whatnot. There'll be all kinds of doin's. But they ain't goin' to change a sunrise on a fine day. No sir, they are not."

He unlimbered his old field glasses, once more blessing the army officer who had bet them in a poker game and lost. He scanned the horizon, stopped, focused. There was the carriage of Demetrius, there was the camp. They had not moved since the incident of the night. The herd did not look fully assembled to Buchanan's expert eye. The cattle had run hard and long after Luis Apache's wolf calls had spooked them.

There were two cook fires. The cavvy grazed on the scant grass. Men moved without spirit, dragging themselves after the rough, tough night. Only Spandau, immaculate in fresh garments, seemed untouched. There was no sight of the boss nor of Bull Skagg.

Buchanan broke out the food prepared by Lulu. He sat cross-legged and ate and drank the cold water and occasionally took another look at the camp of the Demetrius herd. There was nothing to see that was interesting, but he could read their intent. They would rest and reform. They would gather their forces and decide what step to take next.

He leisurely finished his repast, then climbed aboard Nightshade and aimed him northward. They could gain a day on Demetrius and it would be about enough. Buchanan wanted to get to Dodge first and see his friend

Luke Short to learn if any of the cattle buyers whom he knew were still in town. He had ideas which allowed for underweight beef. He had ideas which would at least allow them all to break even and give a new start to Lulu and to Porado.

Porado paused for coffee. He looked at Lu, looked away, and said, "I'm sorry, you know. I could have got you killed."

"You did what you thought was right," she answered. "Buchanan was there. He's always there when he's needed."

"Yes," said Porado wistfully. "He's got the knack. He's always on the spot."

"Don't feel bad," she urged him. "It all worked out. Buchanan says it's all for the best."

"I hope he's right." He swallowed the hot, scalding stuff and asked, "Are you ready to go?"

"Like Buchanan said. Ready and willin'."

He said, "All right. We'll move 'em out, then."

He went to his horse. She emptied the coffee pot, kicked dirt over the remnants of the fire, folded the tripod and loaded it into the chuck wagon, using heavy leather gloves to protect her hands. She saw Luis Apache watching her from the wagon. He seemed slightly amused.

"What you laughin' at?" she demanded.

"Nice man. You not so nice to him, though."

"That's none of your business, you little Indian snooper, you." She was laughing, but she felt herself flushing, too.

Texas Kid came riding on a roan pony and called, "Porado's sweet on Lulu! Why don't you be good to Porado? He can't help it that he ain't Buchanan."

She said, "I'll take a whip to you, young un. You just wait."

The Kid rode off, laughing loudly. Luis gathered the reins and started his wagon. Lu climbed to the high seat and sat a moment looking down at the ears of the team, wondering why she felt warmly toward Porado since he had made that rash ride. It was the wrong thing for him to do. It had also nearly ruined Buchanan's smart play.

And Porado had seen her with her shirt off, too, which made her very uncomfortable.

Still she did feel kindly toward him. He was always so polite and thoughtful. He was like Buchanan that way, considerate of a woman.

Of course he could never match Buchanan. No man could. Lu knew that. Lu had been around the frontier for a long time.

Maybe too long, she thought. Maybe this business of getting a new start was not for her. Maybe the old exciting, dangerous, loose and gambling way was what she should have pursued.

She did not know what drove her to want change, or got her to invest in a bunch of damn cattle she didn't know the first thing about, or sent her up the trail. It wasn't Buchanan. It had started before he had reappeared. And whatever it was, it did drive her. Her head came up, she picked up the leather ribbons and said, "Gee up, there, we're goin' to Dodge City, state o' Kansas."

Buchanan caught them at the nooning—in time for another meal. That was a rarity, two meals hand-running. He was quite pleased. He sat with Porado and told him what he had seen.

"Then you think we ought to make a run for it?"

"No other way," Buchanan told him.

"No matter if our cattle is skin and bones?"

"It matters in a way. But there's other ways."

Porado said, "I hope you know them real well."

"I'm just hopin'," Buchanan confessed.

"Well, best talk to Lu. If she agrees, we'll push."

"Right." Buchanan went to Lu and talked to her.

She asked, "Is that the best way?"

"I can't guarantee it," said Buchanan. "But with all we got against us—I'd say it's as good as any. Maybe better."

She said, "All right. Let's move 'em."

They set Tom Fool in the lead and increased the pace. It was the hardest kind of work. Rebellious cattle broke from the line of march and had to be chased and chivvied back. Some of the older steers broke down and had to be left. The calves were all doomed, none could keep up. They were branded and left with hopes of being picked up on the return trip from Dodge, or that they might be brought in by honest drovers. Buchanan stayed with the others now, driving himself day and night.

It was a hard time and it was a good time. Each day brought them nearer a goal they all now could almost see. There was no longer any bickering; indeed, scarcely a minor misunderstanding. They had learned the ways of each other so that they anticipated every move, like a well organized team.

Every day Buchanan rode the back trail with his guns, looking for attackers from the Demetrius crowd. Every day he returned without having seen them, and helped Coco on the drag where the weaker cattle strayed or lagged and had to be choused into line. The beef dwindled as the pace and the sun took its toll, but the hoofs went forward, one after the other, headed for Dodge City.

The humans also lost weight. Supplies ran low, and Buchanan was forced to shoot tough prairie rabbits and kill an occasional steer for eating. Everyone grew tired of beans and sourdough biscuits. Lu Lacy looked more like a slim boy than an opulent lady of the frontier fleshpots.

Yet they persevered.

When they crossed the border Buchanan took one last ride. He circled wide and took plenty of time. He finally came within view of the Demetrius herd through his glasses. He sat upon a knoll and watched.

They had conserved their strength, he thought. They were riding easy with the supplies they had gutted from Doan's store back on the Red River. They gained a bit on the herd ahead. Demetrius must have a plan, Buchanan thought. It would be a smart one, complete with all the violence pent up since their last encounter.

There was nothing to do but push on and claim a graze outside the town of Dodge. Then Buchanan planned to ride into town, see Luke Short and find a buyer . . . a smart buyer who would listen to reason.

The day came. In the distance they could see the smoke from the chimneys of Dodge City.

There was not another herd in sight. They had all been grabbed up by the eastern buyers and long since shipped. The grass was growing back and Buchanan led them to a high graze which commanded a view of the back trail.

"They'll be in here tomorrow," he told Porado. "Anything can happen once they get the herd bedded down."

"They won't forget," Porado acknowledged. "We'll have to let the boys go to town, though."

"Two at a time," Buchanan agreed. "But first you and Lu and me better shine up and see what we can see."

"I'll tell the boys," Porado said, hesitating, then going to where Dutch and Dude were eating, while the Kid, Luis, and Coco watched the herd. Lu was already dressing under cover of the tarp which had been her boudoir for all the time and all the miles since Fort Worth.

Buchanan washed up and changed to city pants and shined boots and a clean shirt. He wore a soft deerskin beaded vest presented to him by a Crow chieftan. He also wore his six-gun, which was against his practice when he went in to town. His mind went around and around as he tried to figure the first step that Demetrius would take.

Porado appeared, trim and neat in black, a somber figure but smiling. They waited for Lu, growing impatient. Buchanan called to her, "Hey, Lu, it ain't a barn dance, you know. Just a business meetin'."

She came from under the tarp. She was not wearing a dress. She was attired in a fresh man's shirt and clean Levi's, a bit loose around the waist. When they stared at her she grimaced.

"Tried on three outfits. Not a damn one came close to fittin' me. I could spin around in 'em. Lost so damn much weight I couldn't get a job in any dance hall west of the Mississippi."

Buchanan said, "You'll get it back when you settle down to three squares a day."

Porado was looking her up and down. In his quiet manner, he said, "I hope not."

"You hope not? You hate me?" Lu laughed.

"I like you the way you are," blurted Porado. "Slim and . . . beautiful."

Her laughter froze. "Hey! I ain't beautiful. Don't say things like that."

Porado said, "You're beautiful enough for me." He turned away quickly and went to his horse.

Lu's high cheekbones were red. She said to Buchanan, "That dude—he worries me. Beautiful! You know damn well I'm a good lookin' dame but I ain't beautiful."

Buchanan gave her a hand onto the patient dun horse. "Well, there's an old sayin', Lu."

"Tell me all about it."

" 'Beauty is in the eye of the beholder,' " Buchanan said, swinging aboard Nightshade. "Porado, he beholds you in his own way."

She settled into the saddle, watching Porado as he led the way to Dodge City. "He's a strange dude, all right. Real strange. He never even touched my hand all the time we been on this trip. But I seen his eyes buggin' out. I ain't that blind, Tom Buchanan."

"He's a good man," Buchanan told her soberly. "A real fine man."

"Time'll tell." She tossed her head. "I note that you didn't back up what he said."

"Why, sure I back him," Buchanan said. "You're better lookin' now, since you lost that weight."

"You mean I was fat? A fat old honky-tonk dame?"

"Not fat. A fine figger of a woman," Buchanan explained.

"You go to hell."

She spurred the horse and was off toward the town. Buchanan sighed and followed. He had always liked Lulu Lacy. He had made this tough, unprofitable trip mainly— yes, totally—on her account. So what did he get? The edge of her tongue.

But then he had never pretended to understand women.

NINE

"DAPPER" was the word for Luke Short. He was small and he was natty. About five-feet seven-inches in height, he had his clothing hand-tailored in Denver. So neat was he, that he wore his S & W .38 calibre weapon in a leather pocket, especially built so that its bulk would not spoil the hang of his stovepipe striped trousers. He greeted Buchanan and friends in the rear of the long, narrow confines of the Long Branch saloon, which he had recently acquired.

He said, "Lu Lacy, I wouldn't have knowed you. Why you're purely skinny."

"Shut up, you shrimp," she said affectionately. "What kind of joint are you runnin' here, anyway? No wine for a lady?"

The bartender came with wine and whiskey in appropriate bottles and with clean glasses for all. Luke was a stickler for doing things up right.

He said, "Porado—any friend of this pair . . . Drink up."

They all drank, as was the custom of the land, toasting

their fortuitous meeting. Buchanan drained the whiskey and put both big hands on the round table.

"Luke, my friend, one quick question: Is there a buyer left in the town?"

Luke considered. "There was one got drunk in here last night. Business has been bad, like always when the Texans go home. But since I hired Dorinda . . . You remember Dorinda, Tom. From Ogallala?"

"The piano player? Sure, she's a beaut," said Buchanan enthusiastically. "Where's she at?"

"Comes to work at night. She and a couple other gals. They sing and dance a little. Mayor Dever don't like it . . . But that's another story. Strayhorn's his name, big buyer from Chicago. Seems like he was doin' business with Beau Spandau."

"Who?" They all demanded as one.

"Beau Spandau. You know him. Fast gun but a good man with cattle."

"Spandau was here already?" Then Buchanan saw it all. Demetrius had sent his man on ahead, riding a fast horse, with bills of sale, to make certain he would get first chance at getting rid of his herd. "I got to see this Strayhorn pronto."

"Try the Dodge House," said Luke. "He ought to be sober about now. Reckon Spandau got him while he was kinda drunk, though."

Buchanan said, "I'm all kinds of a damn fool for not thinking of that myself. We could have sent Lu on ahead."

"Lu? You got some cattle, Lu?" asked Luke, surprised.

"Lu and Porado, they own the herd I helped bring up," Buchanan told him. "Spandau's boss is Demetrius. They been fightin' us all the way. It's a long story . . ."

"Demetrius is a louse," said Luke. "He tried to buck my faro bank once. Cried when he was beat. Had to lay him out. The man's no kinda good."

"Let's go," Buchanan said to his friends.

Luke was on his feet. "Wait. Strayhorn, he's a funny kinda fella. Let me get him. You rest yourselves and take a few drinks. If it's bad news you won't feel it so much if you relax and take it easy."

129

He waved to them and walked out the rear door. Porado raised his eyebrows.

"That's the famous Luke Short?"

"That's him," said Buchanan. "Sharpest square gambler in the west. Best friend a man could have."

"I'll back that," said Lu. Her hand shook as she poured whiskey for the men and wine for herself. "Demetrius got ahead of us. I smell trouble."

"We been expectin' trouble," Buchanan said. "It's just the shape it comes in that . . . Well, look who's here!" He got up and beamed upon a young lady coming through the door through which Luke had just disappeared. "Dorinda! If you ain't a sight for sore eyes."

"Tom Buchanan!" She ran and threw herself upon him.

She was a small woman with an abundance of black hair piled atop a shapely head. She had a pert nose and large brown eyes. She was thin in the right places and comfortably padded in others. Her hands were exceptionally fine, with long, slender fingers, carefully kept.

Buchanan held her as though she were a doll and introduced her to the others. "Old friend of mine, Dorinda Dare. Best piano player in the country . . . This here's Lu Lacy—Porado. Came up the trail together with 'em."

Dorinda's voice was musical. "If y'all came up with Tom Buchanan you had a time. Around him there is always a time."

Porado said politely, "How do you do, Miss Dare." He seemed quite pleased at the advent of the small, vivacious lady.

Lu said, "Howdy. Didn't we meet in Virginia City a few years back? Wasn't you playin' at the Bucket O' Blood?"

"Why, yes." Dorinda peered. "My goodness, you're the lady dealer! Lulu Lacy, I should've remembered. You've changed, haven't you, dearie?"

"Like you say, comin' up the trail with Buchanan makes for a time. A time of change."

"She lost some weight," Buchanan explained. "We had a few tough goes along the way."

130

Dorinda said, "Luke told me you were in here. Is it something to do with that Beau Spandau?"

"Somewhat," Buchanan said.

Her face darkened. "He promised to come back and get me. Know what I mean?"

"You got no worries with Luke around," Buchanan said.

"But Spandau said he had some men who would take Dodge apart. He said they are Texas boys just dyin' to rip up Kansas."

"All those Texas cowboys want to tear Kansas apart," Buchanan said. "I'll back Luke and the local lawmen against a hundred of 'em."

"But Bat Masterson's gone. Wyatt's not here any more, neither. Mayor Dever's just about runnin' everything," said Dorinda. "It's getting a bit hot for Luke, even."

Buchanan said, "That's bad. I don't like that."

The rear door opened again and Luke ushered in a thin man of middle years whose bloodshot eyes and shaking hands proclaimed that he had enjoyed a good time the night before but was unhappy today.

"This here's Strayhorn," said Luke. His face was grim. "He thinks he bought seven hundred and fifty head of cattle off a lady named Lulu Lacy and a man named Andrew Porado."

"He did like hell!" cried Lu, jumping to her feet, spilling wine. "Lemme see the bill of sale."

Strayhorn had the papers, all right. Buchanan looked at them. Luke Short produced a stub of pencil.

Buchanan said, "Mr. Strayhorn, you watch. Miss Lacy and Mr. Porado will now write their signatures."

They did so. Strayhorn held the paper up to the light. His bloodshot eyes widened. "What the hell's goin' on here? Excusin' me, ladies, but what the hell?"

Buchanan said, "You paid for cattle without countin' heads, Strayhorn? What kinda buyer are you?"

"Drunk," said the thin man frankly. "This cowboy fella, he offered me a terrific bargain. I bought the herd of a Mr. Demetrius, too. Same price."

"Uh-huh," said Buchanan. He was already on his way

out of the saloon. "Demetrius could afford it. He was sellin' seven hundred and fifty head didn't belong to him."

"But how could he get away with it?"

Buchanan said, "He figured to bury any mistake he might have made. Are you comin', Porado?"

Porado said, "Lu, stay here, please? I mean, Miss Dare and Mr. Short will look out for you, I'm sure."

Lu retorted, "And leave you galoots to fight for my cattle? Like hell!"

She was right behind them when they mounted at the hitching rack in front of the Long Branch Saloon. People watched the dust rise beneath them with little interest, believing them to be no more than the last of the trail people who brought prosperity to Dodge—and were despised for all their pains.

Nightshade pulled ahead as always when Buchanan turned him loose. The long-striding black covered the ground like the morning dew. It was they who first heard the sound of shots which Buchanan had expected. He unlimbered his rifle and signalled to the pair behind him.

The camp was already torn apart. The chuck wagon lay on its side and from behind it there came rifle fire. The supply wagon was afire. The cattle were vanishing over the horizon to the north.

Riders circled the defenders in the shelter of the chuck wagon. Buchanan came within range. Rising in the stirrups, he began firing the Winchester. It was neither the time nor the position for good marksmanship, but he wanted attention and he wanted it now.

One rider swerved from the determined path. He threw up his hands, screamed and tumbled from the saddle. Buchanan had got in a lucky shot.

He saw Spandau riding his fancy silver-trimmed saddle, and Skagg on a big red horse. The herd was gone out of sight. Now their problem was to pick off Buchanan and friends one by one or en masse, as the case may be. The forgeries would stand up only if all were dead—or at least all but the Apache boy and the Negro prizefighter, whose word would not be good in the white man's court. It was a rough plan but it could be made to work if all went

132

well for Demetrius and his band. There were, after all, a great many more of them.

Buchanan waited for the others to catch up. He pointed to the chuck wagon. Spandau and his men attempted a charge. Blazing fire met them. Another man went down. Spandau waved them off, out of range. He stared back at Buchanan and his companions, and for a moment hostilities ceased.

Buchanan said, "You see what it is? They made a surprise attack. They tried to burn the camp, they got the wagon. Now our people are standin' them off. It ain't good enough."

"What should we do?" demanded Lu.

"You and Porado, you go in and see who is hurt and if they got the ammunition from the supply wagon before it burned."

"Damn, I didn't think of that."

"Find out how things are with us, if we got horses left alive."

"Where are you goin'?" demanded Lu.

"I got a theory." Buchanan grinned at them. "They never expect you to come to them. Do like I say, now!"

Nightshade was off and running. Buchanan had his second revolver in his belt. The rifle was in his hand. He headed straight for the men sitting on horseback, Spandau, Skagg and the others.

They stared. They seemed unable to move. The spectacle of one man charging a dozen mixed up their thinking, upset all their preconceived notions. Buchanan took the bridle rein in his teeth and drew his Colt's from the belt. He began firing the gun at the precise moment the enemy was within his range.

One man went down. Another howled and went riding off to the west, with an arm flapping. Buchanan came on, getting an aim, trying for the leader, the man sitting the silver-mounted saddle. Spandau wheeled as a bullet clipped his ear.

Skagg was already bent low over his horse's neck, careening away toward the west. The others followed. Spandau trailed them, turning to get off some shots of his own. Buchanan aimed low and Spandau's horse faltered in its stride. Two men fell back. The horse of the man Buchanan had downed was running wild. Spandau roped him. Buchanan withheld his fire in admiration as the cool cattleman changed mounts. In a moment the remainder of the gang was gone from view.

Buchanan rode back to the chuck wagon. Now that the heat had lessened he was worried. Coco was back there and Coco did not shoot a gun, was afraid of guns. The two boys, Porado's faithful, silent pair of followers, had been forced to bear the brunt of the attack.

He dismounted in their midst. Lu was tying up a bloody head. It was that of Texas Kid. Dutch sported a wound in his left arm. Coco stood at the rear wheel of the capsized wagon, trying to remove food from its interior.

"Is that all the damage they did?" Buchanan breathed a deep sigh of relief.

"They shouldn't have done any," said Texas Kid. "They got the herd goin'. We seen 'em, we shoulda stopped 'em."

"No," said Luis Apache. "There were too many. They came too quick. We had to run."

"Retreat," said Texas Kid. "We retreated. Then we began to shoot back at 'em."

"Coco got one. Dragged him down and beat him to death," said Luis Apache in Spanish. "Coco cannot shoot a gun, no?"

"No," said Buchanan. "He does not shoot a gun. He does all right without shooting."

"He is one *hombre*."

Lu demanded, "But what now?"

"Horses?" asked Buchanan.

"*Si*. One for each," said Luis Apache.

"He seen to the horses," said Texas Kid. "Right under their noses. Got 'em over yonder rise. Reckon they thought to wipe us out, didn't bother with the cavvy."

Coco said, "Everybody moved quick, Tom. Everybody did good. I don't think I killed the man. They toted him away. I hope I didn't kill him." He piled cans of peaches and tomatoes, and added a batch of biscuits which Lu had left behind for them. "Should be some cold meat if it didn't get spoiled."

They ate. It was surprising how calm they were, Buchanan thought. The herd was gone, there were men wanting their death, the odds against them were still enormous. He managed a sandwich and a can of tomatoes, never a task for him, then realized they were all looking at him.

He swallowed and said, "This is what it all comes down to. Man wants peace, bring a herd up to Dodge and we get a war. We could try to go for the law and by the time we succeeded they'd be the hell and gone to some place we couldn't find 'em. So what must we do?"

"Ride," said Lu.

"Ride," said Porado. His two men nodded without a change of expression.

Apache Luis and Texas Kid did not even bother to respond. They went over the nearby rise and began rounding up the horses. Lu made packages of food smartly and neatly. The men stuffed their saddlebags. Porado pointed out boxes of ammunition.

"The boys yanked it clear before the fire could get it. Guess there's enough."

"Fill your belts and your pockets," Buchanan said. "If we can get at 'em, it's enough. If we can't, no amount of bullets is enough." He looked at Lulu. "Luke Short's a mighty good friend of mine. How 'bout you ridin' back to Dodge and askin' him to bring some help?"

"You heard what he said. Masterson and Earp and his pals are gone from here."

"Well, anyway, you could try."

She said, "There's an extra rifle."

"But it's no place for a lady out there."

"Some of them cows is mine and besides, like I say, I'm no lady."

Porado said, "Buchanan's right. Bullets don't care who they kill. You ought to go back, Lu."

She faced them in the late afternoon sun, gaunt, grim with determination. "Without the cattle—I'm nothin'. With it, I got a chance for a life. What difference does it make, man or woman? It's my play."

The boys came back with horses saddled. Buchanan looked around. "Any objections?"

No one spoke. If they were unhappy at having a woman in a range war, they did not care to speak up.

Buchanan said, "One thing to remember. I don't want Demetrius killed."

"That son—why not?" demanded Texas Kid. "He's the cause of all this."

Buchanan said, "Just trust me. Don't kill him. If he starts to run, go after him. Capture him alive."

Luis Apache asked eagerly, "You let me handle him? Like our people do?"

"You'll see when the time comes," Buchanan told them. "I got ideas about Demetrius. Now everybody see to the food, their canteens, ammunition, weapons."

The horses were saddled and ready, watered and fresh. The plain stretched far and wide—and flat.

Buchanan said, "They think they're safe. We don't dare ride in while the sun is up. They could pick us off easy. We got to wait until dark. And they'll be lookin' for us, believe me."

Porado nodded. "They'll be looking. It'll have to be something tricky."

"I'll think of something tricky," Buchanan promised. The sun was dipping toward the western horizon. "Let's take it nice and slow and watch out for an ambush. Luis, you ride on my right. Kid, you take the left. Porado, you and your boys stay with Lu. Okay?"

They set out together on their foray against the enemy. They still knew the odds, all of them. They had eliminated a few of the superior numbers but they were still pitifully few—and a woman among them, plus a huge black man who refused to carry a gun.

Buchanan and Luis Apache met afoot. They were between their own group and the encampment of Demetrius. The Indian boy shook his head.

"No can do."

"Right," said Buchanan. They mounted and rode back

136

to where the others waited. They tied up their horses with the rest of them and sat down on the ground.

Buchanan said, "We can't go in on horseback."

"Why not?" asked Porado. "We've got to take chances."

"It would be suicide," Buchanan told him. "Luis and me, we went all around the camp afoot. They got guards every place and they're so nervous they're skitterish. One of 'em almost shot Spandau when he walked too close."

"But we can't just walk in carrying guns and ammunition."

"No. We can't do that," said Buchanan.

"Then how do we manage?"

"We sneak in."

"But how?"

Buchanan said, "They got so many guards posted that there's only two men ridin' herd. And they got a lot of cattle, what with your extras."

"You mean we go in through the herd?"

"I mean we try it," said Buchanan.

"It can't be done!" said Porado.

For the first time since leaving Fort Worth they seemed to disagree with him, Buchanan saw. He waited, letting them think about it. Luis started to speak but stopped when Buchanan shook his head.

Porado murmured, "Well . . . Lu could stay and hold the horses."

"And wait and wonder if you damn fools are gettin' killed? You do pick the spots for me, don't you, friend?"

"You can't walk through a herd of cattle?"

"I'll make it as good as any of you!" she cried. "Damn it, if Buchanan says so, that's the way to go."

"Someone's bound to get hurt," Buchanan admitted. "The herd may not stampede, it bein' worn out some already. On the other hand, it may run down everything in sight."

"That's a chance to take," Porado said. "But . . . afoot? It's not natural."

Coco said, "It's natchel for me."

"Me too," said Luis Apache.

Buchanan said, "All right. Take off your hats."

"Hats?"

"Walking among longhorns with your hat on ain't exactly safe," Buchanan said. "You bend your head and slide through. You have two guns ready, long or short. You fire your long guns from the hip. You try to knock down anyone who isn't wearin' a white arm band."

"Where do we get . . . Oh, sure," said Porado. "We rip up anything white we got on us."

"But we ain't got anything white," protested Texas Kid.

Lu said, "Okay. Everybody turn their heads. I see I shouldn't of wore my good undies under my Levi's today. Imagine, walkin' through a herd of cattle without underpants!"

They hobbled the horses and left them on the prairie.

There was no moon when they began to walk. They paused several times in the darkness to adjust paraphernalia that seemed to be clicking or creaking. Their eyes gradually became accustomed to the lack of light.

Buchanan said, "I'll show you the best spots to start through the herd. Then you go slow and wait for me. Try and wait until one's through shootin' and is reloadin' before you begin. Just try. Maybe they'll think there's more than just us comin' at 'em. Maybe we'll get lucky. From now on . . . we'll need it."

He led them to where the herd was bedded down. They held their breath, lying flat on the ground, as a rider went by, lazing in the saddle.

Buchanan sent Dutch and Dude in at this point. The others walked on. He kept Coco at his side. Luis Apache showed Texas Kid another spot picked earlier on their scout. Porado hung on.

Buchanan nudged him. "You and Lu go in here. You might come out opposite Demetrius's wagon, the way I saw it. Remember, don't kill him."

"Can I wound him a little?" breathed Lu. "I'd love to make him suffer some."

"He'll suffer," said Buchanan. "Get goin'."

He watched them ease their way in among the cattle. He said, "Coco, I know this is goin' to be rough on you.

This ain't your game, not anyhow. Stick by me. If you can get your hands on Demetrius, rassle him around and keep low. It could save both your lives."

"Show me the way," Coco said. "I'll rassle him."

"Shh! Down," whispered Buchanan.

The other rider was coming through, singing the interminable lullaby of the herd. Buchanan found himself lying alongside a big steer. The rider passed and Buchanan ran a hand over the nose and then the horns of the animal. He spoke into its ear.

"Tom Fool? You get up here. Haw, Tom Fool!"

The steer obediently got to its feet. Buchanan shouldered him and, accustomed to accepting orders, he began to shove his way through the herd. Coco hung on the other side, maintaining a low profile. Buchanan doubled over, loosening his two six-guns. He had left his rifle behind this time, knowing it would be battle at close quarters. Tom Fool lumbered on, and now there was some commotion all through the herd at the places where the infiltrating had begun.

It was alarming. It could rouse the defenders. It could cause a stampede, which might wipe them all out before they could get into battle.

Buchanan said, "Tom Fool, you're a good one, but you're too damn slow. C'mon, Coco."

He moved faster. Someone alongside a campfire raised his voice, "What the hell's goin' on there?"

"Damn if I know," said another. "Spandau?"

The foreman came from the carriage of Demetrius, gun in hand. "You see somethin'? Yell out if they come ridin' in, like I told you. We got guns everywhere."

Buchanan spoke from the near edge of the herd. "And we got some guns on you, Spandau. Tell your men to throw in. Tell 'em now!"

Spandau crouched, hand hovering over gun butt. "Buchanan, you sonofabitch!"

Down the line a gun went off. Spandau made his move.

Buchanan shot without careful aim. He hit Spandau in the chest and knocked him backwards. He turned on the man who had yelled and knew he had winged him. They were coming from all directions now. He knelt and began picking them off, trying to keep his shots low. They tumbled like ten pins. Coco strained at his side.

"That the carriage y'all was talkin' about?" he asked.

"That's it."

"Looks like there's hosses hitched to it."

"I'll be damned. The fat yella belly." Buchanan started forward. The carriage lurched and was off. Demetrius had refused to allow the fast team to be unhitched that night.

Porado and Lu were now approaching, bending low. Lu was shooting the rifle, then her pistol. Men were bellowing in the night.

Coco was running. He was accustomed to doing five miles every day in training for a bout. Now he was on the trail of the carriage bearing Demetrius. Buchanan saw out of the corner of his eye that the race would be uneven. He came back to action as Skagg, Monk Morgan, Bowie Gotch and Butch Krause charged in a body, guns blazing.

He saw Porado jump in front of Lu. Even as he fired at Skagg, he saw Porado go down.

Lu, on one knee, cried out. Then she turned loose both her weapons. Krause fell over Skagg. Buchanan shot Gotch. Luis Apache came from nowhere and fired a bullet into Krause.

Suddenly there was a drumfire from another direction. Dutch and Dude had tuned in. Buchanan seized the opportunity to reload, covering Lu with his bulk as he did so. She was shoving bullets into her pistol.

She said, "Porado's down."

"Stay with him," Buchanan told her. "He's too good a man to lose."

"You know," she said frankly, "I'm beginnin' to get that idea myself."

"This may not be the time," Buchanan said. "But if you don't know it—the man's crazy in love with you."

"I'll think about that," she said, cool, calm. "I'll think real hard on it."

Buchanan shot a man trying to get a rifle unlimbered to fire at Coco. The race was over, he saw.

Coco was going over the back end of the carriage. He was ripping the cover from it. Demetrius shot at him twice. Coco ignored the bullets and reached in one arm.

Demetrius came flying out of the carriage. A bit of moon rode out from the clouds and gave some light. Coco threw Demetrius a dozen feet, then pounced on him like a cat on a mouse.

Buchanan shouted, "You better throw down the guns, you men! There's nothin' left to fight for!"

They began to surrender in loud voices. They could see their boss being bounced around like a rubber ball. They could see Spandau, wounded and out of action. They could see Skagg and his bully boys piled up in gruesome awkwardness. They could see the towering Buchanan and his people spaced in strategic positions, ready to cut them down if they did not quit.

A new voice called loudly, "Do like Buchanan says. Any galoot makin' a bad move gets it right in the neck."

A horse and buggy came into view. The man named Strayhorn was driving. Luke Short sat beside him with a shotgun over his knee. Texas Kid and Luis threw wood on the two fires. Porado lay on the ground with Lu beside him.

Buchanan said, "Coco, bring him over here."

Coco put one hand on the burly Demetrius. In two shoves he hurled his victim to where Buchanan waited. Luke and the cattle buyer climbed down from the buggy.

"Well, howdy, Demetrius," Luke said pleasantly. "It sure is good to see you mussed up."

Demetrius began to curse in his native language. Nobody listened.

Buchanan said, "There ought to be a bag with money in it somewhere. You want to look, Coco?"

The well-trained horses hitched to the carriage had stopped when the reins went slack. Coco climbed inside and rummaged around. In a moment, he hauled out a black bag much like those carried by country doctors.

"That's the medicine," said Buchanan. "We'll have a look. Right, Demetrius?"

"You can't rob me. I'll have the law on you. Mayor Dever's a friend of mine."

"Yeah, he vouched for Spandau," Luke Short said. "Nice fella, the Mayor."

Buchanan said, "See if there are some blank bills of sale in there, Coco."

"Yep. Here they are." He held them out by the light of the fires and a lambent moon come from behind clouds.

"Just fine," said Buchanan. "Now let's see. We'll fill these in. Conveyance of a thousand head of Demetrius owned cattle to Lulu Lacy."

"You can't do this!" howled Demetrius.

"For one dollar and other considerations." Buchanan explained to Strayhorn and Short, "You see, he did bad things to Lu. So—considerations'll be fair enough. Right?"

"Anything you say, Tom," Luke assured him.

"Well. Now, damages. What cash is in that there bag will take care of the burned chuck wagon, dead cattle, injuries suffered by our employees. That sound right?"

"It ain't enough," said Short. "Maybe you ought to take some of his hide, too."

Demetrius said, "I won't sign. Nothing in this world can make me sign."

"Take out fifty dollars," Buchanan said ignoring the outburst. "Give it to him."

Coco thrust the money into the coat pocket of Demetrius.

Buchanan said, "Now you can sign the papers. Strayhorn, you got a pencil?"

"Right here."

"No," bellowed Demetrius. "Never!"

Buchanan let the words ring on the night air. He waited a moment. Luis Apache had his sharp knife out. Coco was looking at one big, knotted fist as though he had never seen it before.

Lu Lacy came and stood before Demetrius. "Now there. Remember me?"

"I'll never sign!"

Lu took her .32 calibre pistol from her belt. She held it loosely in her hand. "'You know, I'm the one to do it, fellas." Her voice was cold and steady. "I'll shoot off his good ear first. Right? Then a knee. Then another knee. Gettin' warm?"

Demetrius opened his mouth once more. Then a flare of firelight caught Lu's eyes. He stared into them for a moment. He looked at Luis, at Coco.

His shoulders sagged. He reached for the pencil proffered by Strayhorn. He trembled as he signed the articles of conveyance of property.

Strayhorn spoke. "After I get through spreadin' the word, you won't do any more business with cattle buyers," he told Demetrius. "Your name from now on is mud."

"I'll get you and all of them. I swear I'll getcha!" Demetrius wept. Tears were streaming down his cheeks. He ran awkwardly to his carriage. He stumbled in and grabbed the reins. "I'll get all of you!"

He drove away to the west, away from Dodge City. No one bothered to watch his going.

Buchanan said, "We have to get Porado and the other wounded into town. Everybody turn to, please. Put them in the wagons." He stared at the Demetrius men disarmed, grouped together. There were only four of them left. He went on, "You boys want to work?"

"Anything you say, Mister Buchanan," said a young herder.

"All right, lend a hand."

Lu was still kneeling beside Porado. He was talking to her in low tones for her ears alone. She put a hand on his cheek.

Buchanan said to Luke, "She never even knew his front name until now. Shows what a trail drive can do for people."

"You want a ride to town?"

"In that? Not while I got a horse back yonder. One thing, though."

"Anything you say."

"I'd like to use your office for the payoff. You know,

wages, the split between Porado and Lu. And I got an idea for Mr. Strayhorn."

"What's that?"

"You saw the cattle. Mighty thin stuff, even at the agreed price."

"That's right."

"There's the two boys, Kid and Luis. And Porado's men. Maybe a couple of Spandau's boys ain't all that bad. You could send the herd up to Wyoming where there's grass. Fatten it and it'll bring you good profit."

Strayhorn said, "That's a notion. A good one."

"If you need cash," Buchanan said, "I'm right sure Lu would advance it from the money Demetrius, uh, paid her."

"It can be worked out. You're a good businessman, Mr. Buchanan," said Strayhorn.

"I am? Then how come I haven't got my investment back? Nor my wages from the trail drive? Nor Coco's wages? Uh-huh. I'm a great businessman."

"I'm sure you ain't worried about it," said Luke. "And I got a message for you."

"What kind of message?"

"The best kind," Luke said. "Dorinda says to hurry back, she misses you already."

Buchanan started the walk back to where he had left Nightshade. "You know what?"

"What?"

"I'm beginnin' to miss her, too."